SAVAGE SURRENDER

Also by March Hastings

Abnormal Wife
Again and Again
The Boys of Brigham Dee
By Flesh Alone
Crack-Up
The Demands of the Flesh
Design for Debauchery
Enraptured
Fear of Incest
The Heat of the Day
Her Private Hell
The Jealous and Free
Obsessed
The Outcasts
A Rage Within
Savage Surrender
The Soft Way
Three Women
The Third Sex
The Third Theme
The Unashamed
Veil of Torment
Whip of Desire

SAVAGE SURRENDER

MARCH HASTINGS

ISBN-13: 978-1-952138-97-3

Published by
Cutting Edge Books
PO Box 8212
Calabasas, CA 91372
www.cuttingedgebooks.com

"I cannot love
    ever—
Not you or any
    man—"
She swore,
Denying and Denied.

But I,
Disrobed of my aloneness—
Cloaked in threads of love,
Reached for and
    through
The wordless shell
Of her denial.

—D.B.

CHAPTER ONE

"Watch out for that crazy broad, Chuck. She's out to nail us."

The battered Volks ahead of them chattered and bounced blithely on, kicking up dust in finely powdered puffets that settled thickly on their windshield.

Chuck squinted through its rear window at the back of her neck, long and tan and lovely beneath the stark white of her driver's helmet. He cursed softly and aimed a hex directly to the center of her optic nerve. "You just navigate me, Bubber. I'll do the driving."

"This is one lost rally," Bubber sighed. His plump cheeks sank inward as he watched seconds clicking away on the chronograph sweaty in his palm.

Chuck barely heard him. Somewhere along the twisting road with its jagged obstacles and unexpected turns, his thoughts had shifted from the sport to the vintage Volkswagen. The girl—or woman, he couldn't tell which—drove with a nonchalance that had managed to confound him and at least two other cars that had been trailing her from the start. His irritation had rubbed up curiosity. But there wasn't much he could see. Beside her, a boy with lots of red hair did her navigating with businesslike precision. Chuck could feel that the two understood each other without much talk. And something twinged inside him, poking up comparisons with Eve.

Eve was at the movies this afternoon. *Probably.* She didn't like sportscars or badminton or SCUBA or anything involving sweat or exertion. And he had known it, known all about her when they'd gotten married. That was the hell of it.

"Chuck, go. For chrissakes … go."

The stab of Bubber's anger cut through Chuck's fog. He'd been following the VW automatically. Now he swung his Morris sharply into the curve. They clonked over hidden rock and jounced up close to the rusted rear bumper. The Los Angeles sun stared steadily, pouring in through the hot glass, running sweat in odd designs over their skin.

"How much time do we need?"

"Six seconds," Bubber muttered.

"Here they are," Chuck said evenly. "Six seconds for one nasty navigator."

The Morris stabbed ahead. Hard tires slicked through caked mud. Fenders trimmed dangerously close. As they pulled ahead, Chuck sensed the VW leaning away to give him room. Not out of fear, but from courtesy. And withdrawal. The irritation he'd been growing sprouted horns. As he pulled in front, Chuck shot a quick glance at the driver.

His grim scowl met an amused smile, bowing at him through two glittering blue eyes.

"Now stay even at thirty two," Bubber said in a mollified tone. "Maybe we'll get somewhere yet."

Chuck pressed the aching blades of his wide shoulders against the thickly padded seat. *Bitch … and she's smiling at me yet. Damned bitch let's me come through to win because she thinks my damned male ego will do nip ups otherwise …*

Out of habit, Chuck's gaze fed down to the speedometer, checking out the needle at thirty two. His thick hands hung onto the wheel, fighting against a sudden urge to tear the damn thing out from the floor. He wanted to catch her in the rear view mirror but he couldn't bring his eyes up to meet that bronzed, easy amusement again. All he caught was a fast glimpse of his own sun-whitened hair flopping in a random breeze.

Beside him Bubber shifted time charts and maps, simultaneously squinting across the flattening landscape. "That's all there is," his voice squealed with released triumph. "There isn't anymore. Just keep her at thirty two and it's all ours."

"Yeah," Chuck said. The word came out flat and dry and tasteless.

Then something angry surged in him. His foot trembled on the gas pedal. He could hit speed and throw the race right back into the lap of that mocking face so small and casual. Yeah, throw it right back in her lap, where it really belonged.

Beside him, he felt Bubber's tension rolling itself into a needle point of concentration. Bubber, praying them into a win because both of them needed it for their jobs.

Even for a dame with a mocking face, he couldn't rat out on Bubber. And his foot relaxed again, holding the car steady at the magic thirty two.

Far away to the right, he could make out the clump of waiting watchers, herded like grazing sheep against the horizon. He had always looked forward to the cheers, the bursting ovation as he came slamming home. But now as he squinted through the glare, they seemed like a bunch of grinning morons. And himself—the biggest idiot of them all.

The sun glasses bounced in his pocket. He slipped them over his eyes now, needing to hide the smear of self contempt that had rotted away all joy from this afternoon. Once it had been good-natured fun to joggle through a course like this for exactitude rather than the ripping speed of an ordinary race. Once, rallying had been dear to his heart, part of a casual way of life that gave him food for the articles that earned him his living.

He crossed the finish line, beached the car and strolled back with Bubber to watch the others come rolling in. They would have to wait for their timing accuracy to be acknowledged by the judges. Odors of salt water and car grease turned into a ball of dryness on his tongue. He fished for a cigarette in a back pocket of his twill pants.

Bubber waddled along, jabbering as usual, chuckling to himself now like a record playing on the wrong speed.

Chuck made a decent effort to listen. But then his scanning gaze caught sight of the dusty brown Volks pulling in and he knew, somehow, that he had come back, not for the time check, but for this. For her to see that he could face up to her. It was a feeling that didn't belong in his schedule.

He watched the Volks stop and the red headed kid stretch his long legs out toward the sand. A skinny kid, maybe seventeen, who stretched nervously, too bony and hunching a little like a piece of melting steel.

Chuck jammed his hands into his pockets and jingled change. He saw the boy catch sight of him and it gave him the creeps to see the pale white face break into a grin of recognition.

It wasn't two seconds before the kid was jogging toward him, moving lopsided like a colt that hadn't yet found its legs.

"Mr. Tatum." The boy waved and called in a screech of a voice.

Chuck froze. He knew what was going to happen. Already he could feel the irony of it spreading acidly through his veins.

Bubber said, "That's the bastard who got in everybody's way. Use a leaky pen." He took out a striped handkerchief and wiped through his thinning hair to the pearls of sweat standing like blisters on his scalp.

"Mr. Tatum." Panting, the boy reached them, all of him smiling, his green eyes bright with nervous admiration. "I recognized you right away," he said, walking backwards as Chuck continued to saunter ahead. "Gee, it sure was a privilege losing to you, sir."

Predictably, the bony wrist fumbled forward, its long white fingers clutching his precious time sheet. "Could you maybe…"

"Sure, kid. Sure," Chuck said tightly. He took the paper and the proffered ball point pen. "What's your name?"

"James McDermott. But make it read To Skinny, will you? That's what they call me."

"All right, Skinny."

As he scribbled, Chuck swallowed down the revulsion he felt for this length of physical jelly bobbing nervously around him. And from the corner of his vision, he caught the woman swinging up toward them now with an easy, meandering grace. Her helmet dangled by its strap from one arm. She wore a pale green polo shirt over black stretch slacks. The outfit seemed to casually mention that the body beneath it could win in any contest.

"Mom," Skinny said to her as she reached them, "didn't I tell you he'd sign it?"

The triumph in Skinny's voice told Chuck that there had been a conversation between them. One not quite flattering to himself.

"This is my mother, Chuck," Skinny said, relaxing slightly and beaming from one face to the other.

"Mrs. McDermott," Chuck said across to the woman almost as tall as himself. "You've got yourself a fine navigator here. The race could have been yours, you know."

"Never," Skinny said. "Not against you."

Chuck watched a flicker of appeal move into the woman's eyes. Something that told him not to argue, not to apologize, not to do or say anything that might challenge the boy's conviction. It hinted oddly at suppressed violence.

"Not against you," she repeated Skinny's words, making them sound sincere. She leaned slightly away as though preventing a possibility that someone might try to touch her.

The fake honesty in her voice caught Chuck and held him. There seemed nothing he could do but go along with the game.

"We better get moving," Bubber said.

"You go along," Chuck said. "I want to talk to Skinny for a while. He's got real possibilities."

Bubber sucked in his cheeks. But he didn't argue. "See you in a minute," he said, his voice stiff.

Alone with Skinny and his mother, Chuck suddenly realized that he was staring at her. The neat, dark bun caught in a smooth roll at her neck seemed to stretch her skin with nice balance over good but fragile bones. She couldn't be more than twenty-six, he knew. Certainly not old enough to be Skinny's real mother.

Skinny, jabbering on about the kids at school, didn't need any answers from Chuck to keep the chatter moving. Talk about cars and about sports writing always moved in one of several set patterns. And Chuck felt free to consider the possible subtleties about this woman who drove like some kind of minor miracle and managed to look like one, too.

"You drive very well, you know," Chuck said into the first lull in Skinny's headlong palaver. He looked around the boy to smile at Mrs. McDermott.

"We put in a 1300 c.c. engine," she said lightly. "The car practically drives itself."

"And a double clutch plate," Skinny added. "But she sure moves it like a whiz, doesn't she?"

"You bet," Chuck said. With Skinny there as a chaperone, he felt he could say anything.

"Well, now," Mrs. McDermott said finally, taking Skinny's arm, "I think we've intruded on Mr. Tatum's time long enough. Shall we be going, Jim?"

Chuck knew that she had sensed his thoughts, the growing intensity of his interest. And knew that she would have none of them. Whoever she belonged to had loyalty from her as well as sportsmanship. He would not try, therefore, to detain her, to be more of an obstacle than he had already been.

And yet, he sensed that it would not be for long. That somehow, somewhere, they would meet again, he and this strangely intriguing woman. Meet and perhaps…

Chuck rested his hand lightly on Skinny's shoulder. "Your Mom's got me pegged," he said. "I have to get a move on."

And saying goodbye, Chuck swung his back on the sight of Mrs. McDermott. The brief glimpse of something lovely and desired… yet beyond reach… settled inside him like a seed fluttering to earth.

CHAPTER TWO

Bubber drove them back to the motel, chugging the Morris patiently through the downtown jam of traffic that plastered the broad street with a solid line of glinting metal.

"A bath and to sleep," Bubber said. "This was one lousy, rotten day."

Chuck shrugged. "I've got a deadline."

"Well, don't spit about it. You make your own rules. You want to work? So work. I'm just a loafer and it makes me feel good."

Chuck wished he'd shut up. The back of his head felt like a soggy wash cloth and he couldn't get beneath it to fish out a lead line for the article promised to *Hop Up* on today's run.

"I'll tell you," Bubber persisted. "Eve can make me one of her fancy low balls and you can go cozy up with the typewriter."

"Sure. If she's home," Chuck added irritably.

"It's almost six. She's always home for dinner. You've got yourself a good wife there, boy. Only you don't know how to appreciate it."

"Oh, shut up."

Bubber shut up.

They squeezed onto the freeway and sped out toward Hollywood and the pink Spanish style motel that faced a straggly garden of neglected rose bushes and two lime trees.

Eve's white Chrysler sat parked across the street and Chuck knew that he'd better give up his hopes for an evening of privacy. Whatever niggled in his brain would have to work itself out some other time.

Chuck pushed Bubber down the hall to his own room.

"Eve'll call you when the drinks are out," Chuck said, then pushed open the door to this week's jail that he shared with one so-called loving wife.

The drinks were already out. He could smell the whisky two rooms away. It hit him where his stomach used to live. Where something like mortar churned now, heavy and sloggish with an unnamed anger. Grit lay on him like a second skin, baked and cracking and itchy. Six hours worth. It rolled on his tongue and scratched against the backs of his teeth.

"Chuckie," Eve called. "That you?"

Her voice, sing-song and silly, told him the day's news. She hadn't gone to the movies. Or shopping. Or anyplace. It had been one of those afternoons for her. Of moping around, of cursing the four walls of her fate, of boredom, of frustration, finally splashed on the rocks and swallowed. Eve was one of those people who didn't know what to do about living. At least not between boy friends. He almost wished that she had a lover on the side again so she'd be happy and leave him the hell alone.

"No, not me," he said. "Some other guy." He pulled off his shirt and dropped it across an arm of the foam rubber couch. His back had begun to throb with a thousand gnarled fingers stretching toward his spine.

"My stand-up comic," Eve said, appearing at the doorway. She had taken a shower and smelled too good for her own character, Chuck thought, as he stretched muscles. She wore white shorts and the top of a bikini that revealed an abundance of soft white flesh. Flesh that never got out into the sunshine. Her wide yellow eyes managed to focus on him. They swayed back and forth as though she were watching a buoy in a storm. "Tired, Chuckie?" she said and started weaving toward him. "Here, let momma rub your back."

"No thanks," he said with clipped certainty. "I've got work."

"You've always got work," she pouted, flinging the banner of her blonde hair backward defiantly. "What's so great about work?"

"What's so great about sex?" he shot at her bitterly.

"Ooh ooh, Chuckie's got a mad on."

But it didn't stop her from reaching him and flattening her breasts against his naked back. Her arms circled his waist and clung. "Momma's a good honey," she said. "Now Chuckie be a good daddy."

He felt the softness of her flesh nuzzling him. Memories shot like sparks through the blackness inside his brain.

"Quit this, baby," he said with gentleness. "You don't want to get all upset over nothing."

"What means nothing?"

He felt very tired suddenly. The promises he'd made himself, promises not to egg her on in her madcap rush over the hill, began to dissolve. A wife is to be loved, to be used. And this was the first time in maybe six months that she had been home to welcome him... to want him. As her moist lips circled on his back, Chuck found it hard to remember all the other times. All the boy friends that had made him feel like a faceless body waiting on line for her. He stood quite still, trying to gather all his forces into sufficient strength to turn her off.

She pulled him to the sofa and sat him down, putting herself on his lap. The lilac powder on her throat and chest came off on his fingertips. She moved his hand further down.

"You know I love you, Chuckie," she said, curling herself small to him.

He had fallen for her hard many years ago. Fallen and believed that she was a virgin waiting to be taken out of her misery by the sanctity of marriage. She had made a fool of him. He had believed her, —and she had made a fool of him. It seemed a nice balance of justice that the great Chuck Tatum, hero of kids and men of the manly world, should sizzle up like a fried onion in the he-man's world of sex.

With a sudden burst of denial, Chuck stood up, toppling Eve from his lap.

She bounced hard on the carpet and rolled over.

"You stink," she screamed, rubbing her behind. "Stink stink stink, you miserable dirty louse."

Her shrill words bounced off his eardrums as he stalked into the bathroom and, yanking off his trousers, stepped into an ice cold stream of shower water.

It hit his skin and seemed to turn to steam. The volcano of himself had been stirred and boiled up now to overflow. Chuck knew that nothing he could do would stop it. But he stood there, turning the water on with fuller force, opening his mouth to it, letting it beat against his closed eyelids and drag at his hair. *Work.* The weight and relief of work had become nothing now but a pile of feathers blown away to reveal him, steaming like an animal, wild with a need to destroy, to thrust himself, to release the energies of life that refused to be padded down forever.

Stubbornly he stayed in the shower, palms pressed against the slippery tiles, knowing dimly that he must keep himself locked in until the feeling passed.

The bathroom door banged open.

Chuck knew what it meant.

"Come out of there," she yelled. "Come out or I'm coming in."

Chuck knew the one thing she couldn't stand was cold water. Anything that jarred the nerves. Anything not soft and plush. He stood still, waiting for her to scream herself out.

"Hear me?" she persisted, her voice mounting hysterically. "You come out. I mean it."

Still he didn't move.

Silence...

He could imagine her doll's face, distorted now with consternation. Smudged with tears.

Then the glass door slid wide. Voice rising in a shriek against the icy water, she plunged in and flung herself against him, dragging him down with her in the swirling wetness.

Shivering and hot, he grabbed her and yanked her head back by its mane of soggy hair.

Her bra top came away like a wet label. Water bounced off her breasts, nipping the flesh into hard points. His breath grew shorter, a quick born hunger possessing his body in spite of himself. She wiggled him into a corner of the stall and clung now, needing him to warm her, to protect her from her self inflicted pain.

"Crazy bitch," he muttered.

She was like quick sand, drawing him, little by little choking off his life.

His arms and his shoulders curved around her, making a wall of himself between her fragile body and the relentless water. Of all the crazy creatures in the world that had managed to survive, this one could do it only by siphoning off his strength into her own body. He knew that kissing her, making love to her was playing his own personal form of Russian roulette.

But now he was past caring. Past knowing. The sparking red fury of his need thrust him forward to take her, to make her yield, to erase in one blinding moment of possession the horror of their vampire life together. The softness of her flesh was like a sponge absorbing the last drop of his resistance.

She opened herself to him, sucking breath in hungrily as she clung to him. He took her, shattering the chaos of his need. They were flesh in motion—cleansed while uncleansed—beneath the steady rain of ice cold water.

"You love me," she dribbled water. "You know you love me."

And the water pummelled at his back. He could not tell where the truth of himself lay beyond the darkness.

Finally he dragged her out, rolled her trembling body into a large towel and carried her to the bedroom where she fell promptly asleep, small and drained and smiling.

CHAPTER THREE

"So where's my drink?"

"Look, boy, this is just not one of those days."

"Sour apples?"

"Yeah," Chuck said with patience, "sour apples."

He had changed into clean clothes and combed his hair but the recollection of Eve against him still bit. He knew there was no use trying to work tonight. Crumpled pages lay strewn around the living room where he had made the attempt.

"Better luck next time," Bubber said to himself and pulled the door shut again.

They had been friends for a long time, he and Bubber. At this stage, explanations weren't needed. If anything, Bubber felt too sympathetic, talking up for Eve like a religious grandmother.

As though divorce would help anything. How do you divorce yourself from poison ivy? The best you can do is wait till the cursed thing goes away.

Besides, Eve's good intentions were always there, kidding him along that tomorow would be better. That some day, some place, they would find something in common and begin to build their lives on a solid rock.

And part of it was his fault, too. A steady job. A home to live in instead of banging around the countryside. Children... The respectable way of life that made women feel part of things. You can't expect to go on dragging a girl like Eve without bruising the sensitive nerve ends. She just wasn't the type.

Chuck made scrambled eggs and coffee. When she came to, she would need gallons of the black stuff to slosh away the alcohol.

He dumped the eggs onto a cracked plate and then shovelled them into his stomach dutifully.

Then he went to the portable, rolled in another page and tried again. But recollecting the afternoon only brought back thoughts of the little Volkswagen. And the more he wrote, the more he was telling the story of a skinny kid and his mother…

Ideas… What the hell do you do for ideas when the lousy facts are staring you in the face?

He had no connection in the world with Mrs. McDermott and he wasn't about to have any.

But he couldn't get the woman out of his thoughts. He slid his chair back from the desk and strode out of the house, searching into the night for the comfortable equilibrium of yesterday.

The small town of Hollywood, long ago divested of its glamor, spread out pleasantly in the apron of light. Drug stores, music shops, restaurants bubbled with an evening rhythm. Chuck stopped here and there, for a soda, for a pack of cigarettes, for a package of combs because Eve had broken hers.

But the more he walked, the less he could see what to do with the article that had to be in the mail by tomorrow night at the latest.

It occurred to him that he might write the truth. That he had won the race only through a woman's generosity. But then, he had tacitly promised Mrs. McDermott not to reveal it.

Skinny. That damned skinny kid. What the hell could be so important about him anyhow? His fists knotted with annoyance.

For one wild moment, it occurred to Chuck that he could get in touch with them. Run an article on teen-age navigators. For Skinny, gibbering away this afternoon, had let his address slip. And the numbers stuck out big and bold in Chuck's mental file of assorted facts. He lit another cigarette from a butt and reminded himself with a jab that he was only kidding himself. There was nothing in it for him, after all. It would be like knocking his head against stone to close in on Mrs. McDermott. He had known it this afternoon. He knew it now.

At Hollywood and Vine, he stopped in for a large bottle of aspirin and decided to head back home. No use tramping the streets, fighting this strange desire to start trouble with a woman who wanted none of him anyway.

Besides, he still owed Eve an even break. If he began fooling around with women now, his chances of straightening out their life together would be finished.

He picked up a cruising taxi and went back to the motel, figuring that she would be coming awake soon. And needing him.

His head ached with contrary desires pummeling each other inside his skull. But he managed, when he came into the apartment, to flick on a smile.

The bedroom where she lay all crumpled and tiny was dark. He heard her uneven breathing and knew the foul dreams molesting her. She would come to with a head throbbing as badly as his own. He watched one naked arm fling itself restlessly across the blanket. A small moan escaped her dry lips. With her hair all straggled over her face, she looked like something lost in a war. Like something destitute. Like a bewildered child. Her cheeks in the dim light glowed with a slight flush. She had never been in control of her life. Hardly knew the difference between reality and dreams.

Chuck sat down gently on the edge of the mattress, feeling the old twinge of loyalty that always overcame him at last. Life might be better without her. Certainly less complicated. But something in him did not want to abandon her. Did not want to give up. It was all part of a driving compulsion, the will to win. A force that pushed him senselessly toward some unseen yet necessary goal.

Her mouth twisted in sleep and a whimper escaped. She turned, instinctively hiding from the light.

Chuck touched her shoulder, knowing that it was better for her to come awake than suffer through the tension of her dreams.

"Eve," he said softly. "Eve, baby, open your eyes."

Obediently, her eyelids fluttered up, then closed again, fighting both the pain of waking and the pain of remaining the prisoner of her dream.

"Eve," he said again, "come on now."

She sighed and turned over, her hand groping to find his. Now she opened her eyes and kept them open. The whites were shot through with a gauze of capillaries. Her eyebrows came together as though pressing back unnamed horrors. She glanced about the room and settled finally on Chuck's face.

"Was I too awful?" she said in a small voice that reached toward him.

"Not so bad." He wanted to be cheerful. "I've seen worse."

"In a horror show." Her trembling hand fingered his belt and caught hold of one loop. "I didn't mean to make a fuss. You know that, don't you, Chuck?"

He heard the pleading and knew it was true.

"Forget it." He pushed some hair from her cheek. "Just sit up and dose down some aspirin like a good girl."

"Chuck, I . . . I couldn't help myself. You know I'm not an animal like that. You know it. I just had too much of that damned Scotch. It always pokes fun at my puritanical childhood."

"No apologies. Just sit up. That's a good girl. Open your mouth. Take this water."

He had to baby her. Restore some semblance of security. If he could manage to keep everything in perspective, he wouldn't have to feel sorry for her. It was hell feeling sorry for her. It made his guts freeze over.

"I just don't know what to say," she sputtered on. "A woman just doesn't rape her own husband, does she? I mean, a woman doesn't have to do that sort of thing. Not if it's running smooth between them."

She pulled the sheet up over her breasts and held it bunched at her throat. The aspirin had gone down but she needed more water and swallowed gulps of it, trying to clear a roughness from her throat.

"I said, let's drop it," Chuck struggled with his impatience. He didn't know which was worse, their fighting or the interminable apologies, the ritual of remorse that dragged on and on. They were like two rats on opposite spokes of a racing wheel, fighting like mad to get close to each other, yet always standing still.

He leaned back on his side of the bed and clasped his hands behind his head, staring listlessly up at the cracks in the pink ceiling. They looked like dried out river beds running to nowhere. A musty odor from the impersonal furniture seeped through the scent of her perfumes and bath oils lined up on the dresser. The room was like a cave they had crept into for the night.

Eve rolled in close. She nestled her chin against his collar.

"I want to be good for you," she whispered. "It nearly kills me every time this happens ... Believe me, Chuck."

"I believe you."

And he waited now. Waited for the accusation to creep into her voice. The inevitable question asking him why he hadn't come near her all these months. Why he didn't make love to her the way a husband should. Make the proper advances that would have prevented this animal need of hers from revealing itself so barbarically.

Her warm breath blossomed against his neck. She had decided to wait, he realized. Wait for him to do the apologizing now. The rightful apologizing.

Yet there was nothing he could say that would be honest and hopeful at the same time.

He wanted her, yes.

But he wanted her to be what he had thought her to be, years ago in his stupid innocence.

"Chuck?" her voice crept toward him.

"Hmm?"

"Chuck, I'll tell you what." Her fingertips roamed around the hard edge of his chin. "Let's not lie here feeling sorry for ourselves. Let's you and me get dressed and go out tonight. You can take me dancing the way we used to, remember? We'll pretend the whole thing never happened. And maybe, if we pretend hard enough, it'll go away."

Inspired, she sat up and threw aside the sheets to bound out of bed and toward the closet door.

"I'll wear my new white dress. You haven't seen it on me, Chuck. But you'll like what it does to me."

He watched her take the dress out and slip it off the hanger. She pressed it to her naked body and danced around with it swinging out from her waist.

She looked to him like a broken doll at Christmas, her smile lopsided and hopeful, her bare buttocks dimpled and glowing. That's how it was with her, he knew. No consistency, nothing sensible. Just one crazy dream after another.

And yet, going out with her was better than staying here, risking more of her self-recrimination that would eventually lead to another fight and the weight of futility.

"Swell," Chuck said, managing his own slice of energy. "You get into that thing and I'll go find a tie."

Knotting it quickly, he pushed away the recollection of his article still unwritten. Tomorrow morning he would get up early and have a crack at it before she awoke. Maybe after a night's sleep, his brain would be clear of the junk clogging it now.

After all, she needed a period of making up, of settling herself back into his good graces. So tonight he would make it his business to smooth down all the hackles and calm both their choppy nerves. Some dancing... a nice romantic style dinner with lobster tails. A little chit-chat about how it used to be between them.

The warm glow of memories like a salve over the gaping wound of their togetherness now. All the trimmings.

He was running one of the new combs through his hair when the doorbell rang with two short bursts that meant Bubber.

"Answer that, will you, honey?" Eve called from the bathroom.

"Sure."

If Bubber was coming to collect his drink now, Chuck felt he would smash him.

"Well, what do you want?" Chuck said curtly, flinging the door wide.

Bubber looked like something left over from a rummage sale. His fat cheeks quivered and his lips made a stiff, small doughnut of anger and confusion.

"I told you that Volks would put a curse on us," Bubber said.

"You what?"

"And what's more, doesn't anyone answer the phone in your house these days?"

Chuck yanked him inside and slammed the door. "What the hell are you raving about?"

"I got a message for you, that's all," Bubber said, lifting a half filled whisky glass from the table and slugging the stuff down. "From some damned hospital in Santa Monica."

Chuck clamped his jaws and waited.

"Seems your little red headed boy scout smashed up momma's car tonight. And he wants his hero to come hold his little hand."

"You're nuts," Chuck said matter-of-factly.

"Sure. I wish I was. But while you're locking me in the violent ward, take this address and don't say I didn't warn you."

Bubber shoved a torn piece of paper at him.

Chuck scanned the scribbled numbers.

Then he said, "I got a date tonight with my wife. I'm out. I never got the message, see. You couldn't find me anywhere."

"Sure," Bubber said acidly. "And by next week this time, it'll be all over everywhere that the great hero of teen-agery chickened out on a dyin' kid's plea. Why the hell do you think Babe Ruth signed so many baseballs? To keep his batting arm in practice?"

Chuck grabbed the glass from Bubber and slapped it back to the tablecloth. "I'm not Babe Ruth. I'm nobody, you jerk. Who gives a damn so long as I get the stories in on time and win all the races?"

"Look," Bubber tried patience, "we've been together a long, long time. You don't know what's good for you maybe. But I know..."

"What's all the noise?"

Both men turned to Eve's voice. She wandered in, screwing on the first of two pearl earrings. The dress had made a lady of her. It displayed her small, firm body in a neat but simple package, revealing both passion and restraint like trick lights at a side show.

"He wants to spoil our fun," Chuck said.

"Look, Eve, I'm appealing to you. Maybe Chuck's head is as thick as a pigskin, but you've got sense. Make him see that he's got to go cheer this kid up."

"What kid?"

Briefly Bubber explained the day and its consequences.

Eve listened calmly. "Chuck, I'm surprised at you," she said at last. "Since when do you blow so cold?"

"We're going out," Chuck said stubbornly.

"Well, why can't we stop in on this Skinny first? It'll be a good deed. And besides," she smiled slyly, "I think it'll be fun. How often do I get a chance to see my one and only husband playing Santa?"

Chuck jammed his hands into his pockets and flicked silver against silver. What was he supposed to say? How could he tell them they were throwing him to the lions? His glance swept from Bubber's anxious face to Eve's soft, waiting smile. They didn't understand. How could they possibly?

He finished off the last of the drink that Eve had started and Bubber had tasted. It was just one of those things. You fight hardest when you're down and then the bell forgets to ring.

"Okay," Chuck said. "If that's the vote, let's get rolling."

CHAPTER FOUR

They took Eve's Chrysler. He felt her silent beside him, glowing and tense, wound up for the big show.

"Is he really badly hurt?" she said, like a child anticipating the fall of a tight rope walker.

"How the hell should I know?" Chuck spat.

"I should have heard the phone," she said with tiny remorse.

"How the hell could you hear it when you were out cold?" Chuck realized the cruelty of his stab. "Besides," he said more gently, "we got the message, so it's all right."

It was the best he could do to relieve her of the responsibility. Most likely, the call had come through while she was sleeping and he was out chasing away his temper. They were both to blame.

"Bubber makes a good secretary," he added to smooth things over. "Remind me to fire him."

"Bubber's the only friend we have," Eve said with something of gratefulness in her tone. "He's a real professional at pulling us out of the gutter."

"True," Chuck said around an unlit cigarette.

He wanted to keep up a casual conversation with Eve so that his own tension would not shine through. This trip, after all, was supposed to be an act of mercy. The generous handout of a big heart. Maybe, if a little luck would trickle down from the heavens, Mrs. McDermott would be absent. He hoped for this. Prayed to the devils that watched over him for one chance to do his bit with the kid and let him escape, safe from the sight of her, the temptation of her.

Wind roared in through the open vent windows and made a screaming rocket of the car as they careened between convertibles. He hated the hulking mass of metal in his power. Big cars, like fat men in the ring, lumbered. Good in a smashup but lousy for cornering. He wished that someday Eve would learn to shift and make friends with a smaller car. But wishing things for Eve was a lost cause.

They pulled up to the sprawling brick building, spare and neat in the moonlight.

Chuck wasn't good in hospitals. Didn't know how to be quiet and unobtrusive. His footsteps seemed to beat a drum as they strode down the pale blue corridor to the desk nurse.

"James McDermott," he said to the crisp face above the crisp uniform.

The nurse stopped typing on a card and fingered through a file.

"Are you a relative?" she said.

"Yes," Eve put in, touching her hair.

The nurse squinted at her for an instant, then filed the lie. "That'll be on the second floor, section C."

"Thank you," Chuck said and felt Eve pulling him away.

In the elevator, Eve shrugged her shoulders. "So what were we supposed to do?" she said by way of explanation. "Turn around and go all the way home again?"

He had never known why Eve couldn't manage with the truth but this was no time to get philosophical. He dropped the cigarette, still unlit, and ground it beneath his heel. Someday, somehow, she was going to have to separate black from white. He wondered whether he himself knew which was which any more.

The section nurse directed them and they proceeded past door after door, quieted now by the atmosphere breathing illness, perhaps death down their necks. Eve's dress swished jauntily, her hips unaware that this was a time to be sedate. Chuck buttoned the middle button of his jacket. He knew he looked too damn jaunty himself, dressed in navy and gray. He recalled his distaste at Skinny's physique and felt a little awkward at the way he took his own good health and solid body for granted. There hadn't been any crackups in his life. At least not yet. He couldn't even imagine what it would mean to lie immobilized in a hospital bed waiting for some damned nurse to bring in a pan.

"Must be that one," Eve said, rousing him from his thoughts.

"Must be," Chuck said and his chest contracted at the sight of Mrs. McDermott leaning against the wall, watching them coming toward her.

The glinting flame of mockery in her eyes had burned out. Her hands lay folded across the green silk of her jacket, holding herself steady and upright in defiance of an unseen burden. She seemed taller, somewhat thinner and a paleness came through the sunbronze of her complexion. But her chin lifted instantly when she saw them and she summoned a welcoming smile.

"Thank you for coming," she said softly and held out one gloved hand to Chuck.

Chuck waved it off. "This is my wife, Eve," he said.

"How do you do," both women responded to each other in unison.

"We were so shocked to hear about your boy," Eve said with the sociable grace she could always manage.

Chuck knew it served the double purpose of politeness and camouflage for her instant appraisal of the competition.

"His father's with him just now," Mrs. McDermott answered tiredly. "But I know he'd rather see Mr. Tatum."

"Chuck has always been good with boys," Eve said. She glanced at her watch. "Visiting hours are till eight?"

"Yes."

Chuck said, "We've got time."

"I'll just peek in and tell Jim you're here. He'll try to explain to you about... what happened. But it wasn't his fault. He was so excited after the race. I guess I lost my head when I let him convince me to take the car out alone. He never had much practice cornering with such acceleration."

She was speaking half to Chuck, half to herself, condemning and hammering home her own verdict of self-accusal.

When she had stepped inside the room and closed the door, Eve let out a low whistle. "She talks like a grease monkey."

"She knows about cars," Chuck said, defending her automatically.

"So does the local mechanic. You'd think a woman with her appearance could find something better to do..."

"Not now," Chuck's words whipped out.

Eve's eyebrows rose in mock innocence. "Didn't know she was your type," she said. "Miss Autobahn of nineteen sixty two."

"Please. You can toss those precious pearls later."

Eve shrugged and lapsed into silence, hooking her arm possessively through Chuck's.

He let it hang there, like a dead thing, and waited what seemed hours before the door opened again.

A brisk, sturdy man with graying red hair and rimless glasses came out beside Mrs. McDermott. He wore a heavy tweed suit and carried an attache case of burnt olive that matched his tie.

"Hello, Tatum," he said, thrusting out one strong hand. "I'm Jim's dad and I want to thank you for taking the time..."

"Sorry this had to be the place," Chuck interrupted him, his body contracting away from the Madison Avenue approach that had no business in Los Angeles under a warm, vital sky. He got the picture instantly. The traveling ad man. Older. Prestige. Money, of course. It made him angry that a woman like Mrs. McDermott had fallen for this.

Then Eve's voice added her own touch to the picture and it reminded him that he had no business being angry. No business feeling any opinion at all.

He left Eve to conversation with the man and went inside.

Skinny sat cranked up slightly on the bed, his body lumpy with yellowed bandages that showed above the covers.

"Hi," Chuck said, turning it on light and breezy for the kid while Mrs. McDermott neatened a pile of magazines on the bedtable.

Skinny blinked painfully. His pale complexion had gone yellow to match the ointment that seeped through the bandages. "I'm a crud," he said in something above a whisper.

"Maybe so," Chuck snorted. "But now you know that when you soup up a Volks, you've also got to compensate for tangential lean. Hey, don't you read my column?"

"I'll remember," Skinny rasped.

"You're damn right you will." Chuck fumbled for a cigarette and then decided against it. "And what's more, when you bounce out of this box, you bring that heap around and we'll see about putting it back together again. Right?"

Mrs. McDermott shifted a long magazine beneath a smaller one. "Will you be staying in Los Angeles?" she said without looking up.

The casual question made Chuck go hot and cold across his stomach. His remark had been a flip one for Skinny's morale. And she'd caught him in it. Caught him, too, in the trap of his own wishful thinking. It was like slamming his face into ice water.

It took Chuck a second to blink up from under.

He recalled his earlier thoughts. Of settling down at last with Eve. Of making a conventional, respectable life.

"Yes," he said impulsively. "L. A. is a good place to live for my kind of business."

"Well, then," she said, looking at Skinny now and smiling with a new brightness that he hadn't seen yet tonight. "You've got something to hurry up and get better for."

Skinny squirmed a little, shifting his position and trying to smile. "That's great, Mr. Tatum. Just... the greatest."

The door opened quietly and the section nurse leaned in. "Visiting hours are over now," she said mildly.

Chuck leaned back on his heels, a crazy satisfaction spiralling through him that needed to be considered and filed away maybe sometime.

He started grinning. He didn't know exactly why, but he started grinning and couldn't make himself stop till the nurse escorted him and Mrs. McDermott out of the room.

The thing inside him that felt so good was a blinding force and it took him half a moment to realize that Eve and the boy's father were missing.

Then he spotted them down the length of the hall, seated comfortably together on a bench, their heads leaning close as though sharing an intimate joke.

"That looks cozy," Chuck said.

It was Eve's cup of tea and she had blossomed. A new male face, a casual flirtation made a perfect frame for her elaborate femininity. Her head tilted slightly toward his ear and the masses of blonde hair swung down across the side of one cheek. Her soft bosom heaved with the pleasantries of anticipation. Her legs, casually crossed, displayed the beautiful molding of calf against calf.

"Your wife is a very beautiful woman," Mrs. McDermott said.

Chuck's glance flicked back to her and tried to appraise the tone of voice. She seemed not at all concerned with the possibility of a straying husband.

"Skin deep," he blurted, embarrassed for the woman beside him as well as for himself.

"How deep do you want it to be?" she said lightly.

The mockery had returned to her eyes, giving them depth and luster. Reassured about Skinny, she had returned to the easy, sporting approach that made a game out of life. She was a person, Chuck sensed, who could take her chances and lose with the same grace as she could win.

"Sounds like you're used to these things," he said, taking his own chance that she would be honest with him.

"I'll tell you, Mr. Tatum." She opened her purse and extracted a pair of linen gloves. "There aren't many things that make me lose sleep any more."

"Try calling me Chuck," he said briskly. "It fits better."

She had leaned back against the wall, not anxious, apparently, to join the others. Her lipstick, slightly worn at the center of her mouth, added a touch of sensuousness to her lean face. "First names open doors, don't they," she mused, smoothing the gloves over her long fingers.

"That's the idea," Chuck said with directness. "Who the hell wants to beat heads against closed ones?"

"Well, I can't say you aren't honest."

"Check."

She slipped her purse along her arm and folded her wrists into the crooks of her elbows. "But I'm not an honest woman, Mr. Tatum."

"Chuck."

"You take things for granted so quickly."

He fished out the cigarettes and offered her one, then lit his own as she declined. "It's the sporting blood," he said, blowing smoke toward the NO SMOKING sign in black letters near the ceiling. 'And besides, I needed a chance to…"

"Don't speak about this afternoon again. Please." Her voice cracked a little.

"You're going to go on blaming yourself?"

Her eyelids fluttered but she did not answer.

"Look, let's face it," he said. "We'll be seeing each other. You know that. I promised Skinny and I meant it."

"For his sake?"

"His and my own." Chuck felt her studying him, trying to get past the impassive words to his meaning. "If the accident is anybody's fault, it was mine. I know how kids get hopped up over nothing and I should have dried him off after the race. It was natural for him to go out and try to work a little more jazz into that car."

A little sigh reached him.

"But look," he persisted. "Let's thank the fates that it wasn't worse. We'll both make it up to him. How about that?"

"You're a funny man, Chuck Tatum," she said softly. "And no matter what happens, please know that I'll always be grateful to you for coming to see him tonight."

Chuck shrugged. He understood now that she wasn't about to give in to him. No first names. No innocent friendships. No temptations.

He mashed out the cigarette and cupped her elbow. "I guess we'd better round up the herd."

He walked slowly, giving Eve a chance to see them and arrange herself into an attitude more appropriate for the hospital setting.

In sex appeal, there was no contest between the two women. But where Eve was all warmth and capitulation, Mrs. McDermott was all stubbornness, all fire. And the fire was burning something into his brain. Indelible letters spelling out the headlines of his desire. Studying Eve, he knew that her good intentions toward him could be blown away by the hot air of another man's compliments. He wondered, with new clarity, what the hell he was fighting to save with her. What kind of life they could ever make together.

"Time's up, folks," he said with a small thrust of bitterness.

Eve's head jerked, as though she were coming up for air. Her yellow eyes sparkled catlike and secret tive. She could barely hide her annoyance at Chuck's intrusion.

Mr. McDermott stood quickly, guilt rolling easily from his accustomed shoulders. A neutral, hearty smile masked whatever thoughts he'd been contemplating toward Eve. But the shimmering glasses enlarged his eyes a trifle. And Chuck could see LUST spelled out clearly in them.

"Did you have a good visit?" Eve said, shattering the hard shell of Chuck's thoughts.

"Yeah," Chuck said with poison on the tip of his tongue.

"Jim worships your husband," Mrs. McDermott added. "That's the best medicine there is."

"So, Tatum," McDermott lay a hand like a dead fish on Chuck's shoulder. "Your'e the real doctor around here, are you? I want the honor of buying you a drink on that."

"Thanks," Chuck managed. "But my wife and I have a previous ..."

"Nonsense," McDermott thrust, "I won't hear of it. A man doesn't fly in from New York every day of the year to find such generosity and ..."

"We might as well, Chuckie," Eve said as though she had been beaten into it. "And Barney knows all the high spots we'd be most likely to miss."

Barney? Chuck surpressed a sour smile. In the face of such odds, Mrs. McDermott couldn't possibly maintain her moral aloofness very much longer. He wouldn't have to do a thing. Only let Eve play her usual game. It wouldn't take the night before Barney was drawn and quartered, stretched out on the back of Eve's fragrant but deadly bosom.

"Well, man, you can't spoil the fun now," Barney said with triumph.

Chuck glanced across at Mrs. McDermott. He kept his face noncommittal.

"I'd like to go home, if you don't mind," she said mildly to her husband. "It's been a gruelling day."

"Been tough for all of us, that's for sure," McDermott answered as a handout of commiseration. "But girl, you can't let yourself sink into the pit. Up and at 'em. Tomorrow's another day. Jim'll bounce out of that bed as good as new. We have to cheer him on, don't we? Smile, Robin. Give your husband the opportunity to show his gratitude to these two decent people."

Barney had put it in a way that she couldn't refuse without seeming selfish.

Chuck hung on. His knuckles grew white as he clenched his fist against the temptation to push in the efficient, lying face.

"I suppose I am being a spoil sport," Robin said, summoning a smile.

"And you'll enjoy the change," Eve said with double meaning. "A woman has to have a change now and then from unpleasant realities."

Chuck knew he'd better ignore Eve's comments for the rest of the night. She had come here looking for enjoyment, for amusement. And amusement she had found. Somehow, Barney seemed just her speed. Sporadic, insincere, superficial, and the prisoner of his own desires.

S for Stupid, Chuck thought and included himself among the headlong divers into disaster.

"We'll use our car," Eve said and no one bothered to disagree.

As though to put the sarcasm of her intentions into italics, Eve came over and attached herself to Chuck's arm. She gazed up into his eyes, all happy innocence. Her perfume had begun to settle in. An odor of flowers rose from her, suffusing, enticing, promising.

Chuck knew the routine by heart. He felt sick to is stomach. She was acting like a puppy in first heat, swishing her tail in front of the boys, as though riven by a nature stronger than herself, a nature of which she was unaware. He would have slapped her behind if he could. And dragged her home to let her soak in the cold shower where she belonged.

But like Robin—so that was her name—he was wrapped by a responsibility. Robin, at least, had the excuse of her kid for hanging on. He wondered for the millionth time what in hell he was using for an excuse.

They piled into Eve's Chrysler, with Eve insisting that Barney drive. This, too, was part of her routine. The build-'em-into-a-he-man angle that never failed despite its stupid bluntness.

Well, he would let her have her way. Let her pull herself tight on the rope till it finally choked that beautiful neck.

Beside Robin in the back seat, Chuck leaned against the door and watched her looking out the opposite window at the moon gazing at its own reaction in the gentle waves of the Pacific. A damp breeze lifted one random strand of the dark hair. She seemed miles away from the pattering chatter. She clung by two fingers to the side strap as though hanging onto a last branch before dropping over the cliff.

Barney drove slowly, his mind on other things than the traffic, and the car wheeled annoyingly down the center of the road.

"How about something small and cozy to start? Barney said more as a statement than a question.

And a few minutes later, they pulled up behind bar that had been built right into the beach.

The place smelled of beer and fish. Nets hung from the ceiling making the only quiet pattern in the blaring, crowded room. People in bathing suits and shorts clustered four deep at the counter. Crowded tables were lumped around the walls, leaving a small area for dancing.

As Barney led them through the wide doorway Chuck heard Eve whisper to him, "This is *evil.*" And she giggled with kittenish delight, shuddering close to him in a pretense of shyness.

A waiter at the end of the room recognized Barney and stood on tip toe to wave to him.

Chuck saw the limp wristed motion and the rising, tweezed eyebrows. He realized with dry boredom Barney's taste for fun.

The waiter scampered through the crowd and taking Barney's arm protectively, brought them through to an empty table.

"Cute as ever," Barney said, pinching the boy's cheek and winking slyly at Eve.

When the waiter hurried off with their order Barney said, "This is a fairy nice place."

Nobody laughed except Eve, who had to force it.

"Shall we break the boy's heart and dance?" Barney said to her.

For answer, Eve stood up and raised her arms toward him, looking like a Roman statue waiting to be transported.

Chuck watched them move to mingle with their bodies swaying intimately.

"I guess that leaves us," he said, "to make polite palaver."

Robin searched her purse and found a cigarette case.

"Thought you didn't smoke," Chuck said.

"I just don't break rules, that's all," Robin said blandly.

"With that attitude, you could be difficult."

"Of course."

"Well, let's face it, friend. We are two lone monkeys with the same sob story. I'm making a pass at you right here and now, Robin, and if you turn me down, there'll be another day, another race."

"I'm turning you down," she said bluntly.

"Fine." He took her cigarette and rubbed it out in the ash tray. "But in the meantime, we might as well join them on the dance floor before I kiss you."

"Don't be such a big shot." She made no move to get up. "You're in love with your wife. Any fool can see that."

"And you?"

Robin measured him before answering. "Your life doesn't appeal to me in the least," she said quietly.

Chuck flopped back onto the chair. "Come now," he said too calmly, "you're not going to tell me that Barney brought us to a place like this for your sake."

"Barney seldom does anything for anyone's sake but his own."

Chuck moved away the glasses of water between them, lining them up like soldiers. "That's not answering me," he said.

"Frankly, it's none of your damned business."

Chuck threw back his head and burst out laughing. The incredible stubbornness intrigued and titillated him. But he knew also that she wasn't exactly dropping him off the deep end.

"To keep the honesty hot and heavy," Chuck said, leaning forward to touch her gloves folded on one end of the checked cloth, "I think you're flirting with me in your own peculiar way."

"Do you?"

"Mmm hmm."

"Then you're a fool," she said briskly, her eye tightening at the corners into disdain.

"I guess that's nothing new," he said, tilting his head toward the dance floor.

"If I were you, Chuck Tatum, I'd stick to sports and writing. There's something you're really good at."

"Thanks for nothing," he said with an unexpected burst of annoyance.

"Oh, but I mean that."

"Well, you don't have to tell a fish it can swim."

"But I can toss a nice one back into the water."

"All right, friend, I give up." Chuck crossed his hands on his lap. He was beginning to feel a tight ness in his collar pinching the skin beneath. It was a familiar symptom. In a minute he would be getting angry with her. Try to force her to square with him. But her face, so steady and cool in the smokiness, wouldn't scare easy. He was too accustomed to Eve. Eve always broke after three strong words. But not this one. She could dangle him on the end of her line... not throw him back into the water at all. "No more razzing from the bleachers."

"Thanks."

"Now, will you dance with me before the crowd here begins to think we're queer, too?"

He saw Robin smile with acceptance.

Steering her to the dance floor, putting his arm up along her back, feeling the touch of her hand to his, Chuck got his first opportunity to assess her as a woman. She moved easily in his arms and lightly on her very high heels. An odor of shampoo came fresh and pleasant to his nostrils. He drew her in a bit closer, almost by accident. The rhythm of the music in her body needled him with its cry. He felt the tight package of her body keeping its secret wrapped away. Her wide, firm breasts touched his chest lightly, with an aloofness all their own. He knew, he just knew that if he could get his hands on that flesh, it would give to him. Give.

Something bumped him hard from the rear and he swung around to see Eve smiling and nodding over Barney's shoulder.

"Enjoying yourself?" She sounded a trifle shrill. Her hair, no longer neat, flagged the sign of her growing abandon.

Hunched in close, Barney drove her in an intent circle of a repetitious two-step.

Chuck nodded at her, wanting to placate and drive her off, abandon her to the wolves where she liked it.

He put his head close to Robin's ear. "You know what," he said gently. "I'm going to do you a favor."

"What?"

"Drive you home so you can go to bed and forget today and tonight ever happened. They'll never miss us."

He had expected her to argue. At least at first. But instead, something in her body slumped toward him with gratefulness and he heard her say in a very small voice, "Oh, please."

CHAPTER FIVE

Chuck took her home in silence, considering it the better part of valor not to make phony conversation.

He wound the bulky mass of Eve's car up through the dark, twisting path to a low house set snugly into the side of a hill. Through the shadows, he could feel the comfort and conventionality of the plush, residential district. Palms rustled heavily, their thick fronds bending and swaying beneath the lights of a brilliant sky. The clear air seemed to hit his head and he glimpsed the advantage, the security so necessary for a married woman with a kid.

"Come on in," she said at the door, "and have a drink."

Her invitation surprised him. "Asking for trouble?"

"You won't make trouble."

She sounded so definite that he didn't know whether to take it as a compliment or an insult.

"Besides," she said, smiling, "you'll need some fuel to face up to your charming little wife."

Chuck didn't bother to disagree. Robin had Eve pegged. Why try to hide it?

He stepped into a massive room, saw one leading to another through a maze of ornate furnishings. The Oriental rugs and Tiffany lampshades hardly seemed like Robin's taste as he followed her through to a palm enclosed patio that looked down across the hills onto the spread of Los Angeles county.

A barbecue cart beside the oval swimming pool held bottles of whiskey and gin.

"Would you mind?" she said, motioning to it and settling herself into a lounge chair. "And fix me a gin and lime."

Chuck made the drinks, handed Robin hers and strolled along the pool's edge. He felt like he was walking inside a drunken dream where nothing could ever make sense. Finally, he sat down on the concrete, rolled up his pants, took off his socks and shoes and dangled his feet into the water, splashing lightly with his toes. Maybe it was funny, all of this. Maybe he wasn't supposed to file things and believe there was any kind of order or truth when it came to desire.

"Go on in," she called from the other end.

No sense at all.

"Join me?" he said.

"Why not?"

He took his clothes off, knowing that she was doing the same. But he wouldn't give her the satisfaction of turning to watch. He could hear the soft sliding of a zipper; could sense her straining for an out-of-reach hook; could even imagine the lithesome body bared in the darkness. He slipped into the water and let its warmth enclose him as he bubbled downward to the lights that shimmered upward from the flooring.

He frog kicked, skimming along the bottom, and glided up at the deep end where she floated, water lapping over her freed breasts and gurgling across her flat stomach. All of her was as tan as her face. A sun worshipper, accustomed to nudity, unashamed. He spouted an arc of water and turned onto his side, stroking to pull beside her.

"Settles the nerves, doesn't it?" she said wetly.

"Not mine," he answered and dove off away from her, only to return again for some answer, some clue to the meaning of this person so close and yet so far away from him.

But she swam in silence now, working off her own tensions, resting her burdens on the turquoise water and blinking at the sky.

What can a man do?

Impulsively, he reached for her and dragging her down with him, pulled her tight against his body.

She did not struggle.

Weightless in the water, they bobbed to the surface and he pulled her to the side, where, clutching the edge with one hand, he held onto her tight. Pressing hard, he felt a wealth of warmth envelop him.

He spread her lips with his tongue and held her quite still, encircling her legs with one of his own. They bobbed and floated. Her hair came loose to fan out on the lapping water. She tasted of chlorine and he sucked at it with a strange, greedy craving, feeling the sharp evenness of her teeth, the warmth of her curving tongue, the long, smooth line of her swaying and slipping back and forth along the length of his chest, belly and thighs. He took her slow writhing for passion, lowering his lips onto her firm breasts.

"Are you going to take me," she said, panting, "right here?"

"Why not?"

"Mess up the water."

"Care?"

She laughed against his neck. "It's your orgasm."

She was pushing him away. Not with her body this time. But with her feelings. Daring him, almost, to watch himself leaving her cold.

"Come off it," he said roughly, still holding her, certain that she did not really want to escape him.

"Go ahead then," she said, "before you burst."

He let go of the pool's edge and slapped her, stinging hard. Her head flipped back.

"I don't need handouts," he snapped. "Not anybody's. Not even yours."

"M-e-n," she said low. "Is it any wonder that women hate the species?"

"You don't hate it," he said, still holding onto her with one arm. "You're begging for it, only you're too damned proud to let it show."

"Hah."

"Hah yourself."

He felt sure of her. So very sure. Sure because through it all, she had clung to him, nestled somehow against his chest, crying like a baby bird for help without knowing that she cried. Even now her body burned and throbbed against his.

Now he felt her begin to shiver. He got them to the shallow end and dragged her out.

The cold air hit them hard.

He tracked with her through the house to the closet filled with towels in every color and wrapped one around her, as he had done with Eve earlier in the day.

"There's something about women that's all the same," he muttered. "They all need somebody around to tell them how great they are, but they never want to do anything to deserve it."

"So get the drinks," she said calmly, "and shut your fool mouth."

He padded back toward the pool, a towel wrapped around his waist and dangling toward his calves. It was a foolish night that shook up destiny and scattered it with great indifference.

Carrying the two glasses, he returned to find her bending over a phonograph.

"Music?" he said. "Now, how the hell do you expect to fight with me if that damned thing's blasting?"

"No more, Chuck," she said softly. "You came close but you didn't move me. I'm sorry about it. I really am." She slipped a pile of discs onto the turntable. "But I tried to tell you, didn't I, that it couldn't go anyplace between us."

Chuck swallowed his drink.

"You didn't give it any chance at all," he said evenly. "And God forbid, if you did let me and you discovered that you liked it, you'd probably have to kill yourself in the morning. But that's your worry, sister, not mine."

He had dragged in his pants along with the drinks and now he started into them.

"Thanks, Chuck, for not pushing."

"Yeah, thanks for nothing," he snorted.

In half a dozen seconds, he had his clothes on and shot the car down through the narrow road heading toward Eve's glowing, passionate face.

He knew what he looked like with his damp hair slicked back, his shirt open and his pants rumpled. But it made no difference. And besides, the truth was the truth. He didn't give a damn if Eve walked out on him this very minute. As far as he cared, all women could drop dead right now and he wouldn't feel any loss.

Back at the bar, he squinted through the smoke clouded air and sauntered around the edge of the room, feeling vagrant hands move across his backside as he circled for the undesirable sight of Barney slung around his wife.

"They've left you, dearie," a high voice tittered into his ear. "Go for sloppy seconds?"

As Chuck realized the truth in the nasty comment, he also realized a tremendous relief. His whole life had suddenly become simpler than he had ever known it to be since the beginning of his marriage.

All he had to do now was go back to the motel, leave a note for her with some money, pick up his typewriter, and check out of her life for good.

CHAPTER SIX

Bubber met him in the lobby. He flung down a tired magazine and bounced up from a chair to intercept him.

"Get out of my way," Chuck said. "There's nothing left to protect. All I want is to pick up some things and get out. I won't even try the bedroom door."

"Ah, have a heart, Chuck. It's been a rough day. All around."

"Sure has. And I'm getting off this wagon. Tonight."

"Look, do me a favor, will you, buddy? Go around the block and come back again in about an hour."

"I said, get out of my way, boy, or I'll have to bust your sappy face in."

"I don't like to see trouble between my friends. Don't make me choose sides."

"Choose nothing. Just move."

Bubber remained like a tree trunk solidly planted before him.

"You asked for it," Chuck muttered.

His fist connected with the flab that was Bubber's jaw and the heavy body sprawled like melting butter.

A squeak came from the desk clerk.

"He's got enough fat for three more of those," Chuck said. "Help me get him onto the sofa."

Together they dragged the unconscious Bubber onto the cushions. A tiny smile tinged his lips.

"See, he really needed a good night's sleep," Chuck said.

Then he took off across the worn carpet and jumped the stairs three at a time, racing for the second floor landing and his appointment with freedom.

They hadn't even bothered to shut the bedroom door and the mattress squealed in Chuck's ears like a stuck pig. There were moans and sighs and the intimate sounds of flesh meshing flesh. He could picture Eve's body straining... sapping the others... demanding what none could give. He peeled off fifty bucks, scribbled the number of his lawyer in New York which Eve knew anyway, grabbed his typewriter and slammed out again faster than Barney could disengage himself.

The Morris waited for him, small, eager and welcoming... like Eve once had waited, he thought with a sour grin. Before they were married, if not after.

Chuck heard himself whistling something as he rattled off to a hotel and realized that his life, in having turned upside down, had finally turned right side up.

Responsibilities still waited.

He had the article to do.

And a snorkeling trip with the Sea Cresters.

His schedule, in being so tight, left no time for foolish women. From here on in, it was going to be dames who wanted it and knew how. Good Daddy Chuck was dead forever.

As kind of a celebration, he checked into a fancy hotel with lots of lights. He wanted a room larger than all three at the motel. With a clean untouched bed that he could rumple up himself. Maybe bring a broad in later on.... After the article got written.

Alone with the typewriter, the first two pages came fast and easy, words moving out of him with new, driving energy. Beside him, a clean drink sat on a clean tray, brought up by a clean bellhop. The air conditioner hummed pleasantly. From beneath the shades, he could almost whistle down to Wilshire Boulevard. Practically call himself up a playmate any time he wanted.

Yeah, life from here on in was going to be a ball.

The typewriter clacked furiously, the keys seeming to move along a magnetic line of force.

He thought of Bubber coming to and trying to smooth things out with Eve.

But the con game was over. And Bubber, too, would have to learn that you've got to choose sides. Then win or lose as the chips happened to fall.

That had been the trouble up until tonight. He'd been playing all ends to the middle. Trying to make a go of life with Eve and trying to live his own life at the same time. And Robin ... Robin had shown him up for the egotistical jerk he'd been. If he had accepted "no" from her in the first place, she wouldn't have caught him ... with his pants down.

Chuck balanced on the two back legs of the chair and had a good laugh at himself. The balloon hero, all stuck with pins, had fizzled out mighty fast. It was time to reconnoiter. Start making sense again. Pull his days back into a pattern that made some kind of sense.

He phoned for room service, gave his pants to be pressed and ordered another couple of drinks.

Then he thrust himself into the job of finishing the article and stayed with it until the end.

It was three thirty by the time the last page rolled out. His neck ached from the effort but the rest of him felt light. He bounced onto the mattress, telling himself that sleep would be a good thing now. But sleep wouldn't come. Something stubborn in him remained crazily wide awake. The clock that ticked inside him, relentlessly, told him that it was early still. Early in the night. Early in his life.

He dressed again, slid the manuscript into its waiting envelope and went downstairs to send it off.

A nervous, drumming tattoo beat out patterns against the back of his head. He kept hearing the lousy, rotten squeaking of that mattress like the shrill laughter of a witch making fun of him. And he kept feeling the wet, stinging sensation of his palm against Robin's cheek.

For a winner, he had come off looking mighty bad this day. He needed something to neutralize it. Something to rack up points for his side.

He strolled into the plush bar where a couple of late hangers on leaned on elbows or stared at themselves glumly in the long, rose-tinted mirror in front of them. Waiters polished glasses and set them upside down getting ready for closing time in half an hour. All jump had subsided. The dinner tables behind the blue velvet rope wore their blank, white faces of cloth, sleeping like fish with round open eyes. The distant ring of a cash register popping drawers seemed to mark the last round of the fight. He hoisted himself onto a stool and called for a scotch, neat.

The waiter slid it to him with a springy movement of thumb and forefinger.

"Say, where do the live ones go this time of day?" Chuck said off-handedly.

He sipped at the drink, letting the small man size him up from beneath black, heavy eyelids.

"Not your town, is it?" he said, wiping the backs of bony hands on a towel that hung from a black cummerbund.

"Strictly New York," Chuck said.

"Angelinos live different."

"So I've heard."

"You know how it is," the waiter said, spilling ice cubes from emptied glasses into a steel drain. "We got cleaned up a couple of years back..."

"Yeah," Chuck said, letting it come through that he wasn't swallowing the stall. He plastered a ten spot to the counter and studied its engraved face. "Guess it happens every election," he said, not looking up at the man. "But that doesn't have to stop people from being friendly, does it?"

A round man, heavily weighted with liquor, rolled off his chair, caught himself on the bar's rim and hanging onto either side of his bow tie, lurched toward the door.

"Want a refill?" the waiter said.

Chuck shook his head. He took out a single for the Scotch, ignoring the bill lying wet on the counter.

The waiter took the single and the ten, slipping the bill toward his palm with the movement of a card sharp. "Guess you can try a place on Alvarado Street," he said. "But I'm not promising anything."

He muttered a number and Chuck filed it. "Thanks, Mac," he said. "And look me up when you come East."

"I like it here fine."

Chuck swung off the stool and headed for his Morris, shuffling through his ideas of how it felt to like someplace fine. He'd been traveling around ever since he was a kid. Six months school here, eight months there, till he cut out on his dad and the pots and pans business to carve his own road to hell.

He slammed the car door and started up the motor, feeling reflexive satisfaction in the sound of well greased parts playing the faithful servant.

"Betsy, let's roll," he said, patting the dashboard and slipping the sawed off stick shift into gear.

Chuck felt himself revving up along with the car. The motor inside him straining on all cylinders to run flat out.

Alvarado Street, wide and deserted looking, appeared to be a bum steer. But he pulled up diagonally across the way and walked around it for signs of life upstairs and down.

He heard something that sounded like a saxaphone and changed his mind about going back to push the waiter's face in.

The door opened to his knock and a girl with streaked braids took twenty dollars from him in exchange for a ticket of admission.

"This better be good," he said to her and walked past her answering wink.

A sweetish odor pricked at his nostrils. He felt like he was dropping into the center of a bubbling volcano crater as he stepped down to the large, bare room, its atmosphere subtly charged, vaguely hazy, and moved along by a live trio of sax, vibes and snare. The music melted and tingled like peppermint. It seemed to chase after the drugged lassitude of the listeners, nudging them occasionally awake.

Someone lifted a white paper with powder wrapped inside. "The first one's on the house," the woman said.

"Not my style of coke," Chuck smiled and turning on his heel, started to leave, cursing the waiter's idea of what he meant by live ones.

But then he heard a familiar giggle. It poked at him from the shadows beside the sax. He swung around again. His gaze knifed through the heavy hot air.

Eve sat at a table, her head against the wall, rolling from side to side as she laughed at something he knew wasn't funny.

His nails bit into his palms.

She had tried every stupid thing there was to try in this world. But never before dope. Never a kick that could turn into a coffin. He felt blood scooting around his temples, bursting to get through. His curses turned obscene, roaring through his guts.

But she was none of his damned business anymore.

He had turned her off just a few hours ago.

Turned her off for good.

And while he thought this, he was pushing his way between the tables, beading in steadily on the black target of that giggle.

"Hey, wait a minute," Barney said, standing up with indignation as Chuck lifted Eve by her armpits and dragged her around the chairs to face him.

Chuck ignored him. He hooked one arm around Eve's ribs. Her body collapsed against his chest. He heard her laughing softly, sharing a funny, funny secret with the pocket. She hardly recognized who was holding her. Chuck knew she didn't care.

"I said, you let go of that woman."

"Shut up, jerk," Chuck said, "before you get yours."

Barney's glasses clouded over with sweat. With an effort that splotched his face red, he sat down.

Chuck, lifting the smallness of her, trimmed around the tables, his lower lip wet with a spike of blood that had burst through from the anger he was fighting to control.

He dragged her across the street and dropped her into the front seat of the car. She folded backward, like a suit being taken home from the cleaner. And the giggling kept up its steady, senseless bubble, her breasts jiggling in response to the vibration of some sordid dream.

There was nothing to say to her. She wouldn't hear him. He could only drop her at the motel and let her wear off the *high*.

A cool calmness had toned down the night's wind, diluting the sky with its prelude to dawn. He drove along, going slow now, feeling the rat race of his life turning into a sour burlesque. The blithering mass of flesh on the seat beside him was enjoying itself in its own crazy world. Only somehow, he didn't know how, he too must be part of that world. And he asked himself where all the good intentions had gone. Where the new life he had peeped into for so brief an hour.

Back at the motel, he lifted Eve into his arms and carried her up the stairs past the desk clerk who knew better than to ask questions or even mutter a cry of surprise.

He passed the door of Bubber's room. It stood ajar and Chuck glanced in to see the emptiness and knew that Bubber had scooted out. The why, he could understand. But the where, he couldn't even surmise. He could only feel that Bubber must be hanging his head someplace, cursing himself out for doing such a lousy job of keeping the lousy play on stage.

In their own rooms, Chuck dropped her onto the rumpled bed. Its grayed sheets and lumpy mattress had seen too much action for one night. Eve sprawled out on it, her dress awry, revealing the curve of one swelling breast. She seemed strangely at home, a dead thing on the battlefield of her passion.

He realized that he didn't dare leave her alone. Not until she came around and he could pack her off on the first plane to New York. It seemed a grinning quirk of some satanic fate that of all the places in this sprawling town, he would have inevitably to run into Eve. It was his fault and the town's fault and no-one's fault.

She moaned and chuckled and blinked at him with hard, tiny pupils fighting against the light of reality.

He pulled up a chair and sat down to wait, staring out the dusty window at the first violet signs of day.

The sun climbed slowly, expanding itself over the low line of houses, slipping its golden warmth around the tall, feather duster palms, radiating pastel shades through long daubs of cloud. Sounds of traffic began to unleash dissonant squeaks, coughs and rattles, pulsing into a lifeblood of daily routine. A bus chucked up hot bitter fumes. A kid's voice yelled, high and happy, in response to another kid. The ribbon of the world rolled onward, tying human fate into a high priced package. Chuck's self-wind watch sliced eight A.M. off the round pie of time. In New York now it would be slushy with the dull muck of winter. He felt here and there and everywhere, tangled into the wheels and caught in the works.

"Ooh, my stomach."

He heard Eve's voice turn into a retching sound. Her body convulsed and curved round itself like a frightened caterpillar. She leaned over the edge of the bed, her complexion snapping into a greenish white.

Chuck brought in a deep pot from the kitchen and held it beneath her chin, massaging the back of her sweaty neck with his cold fingers.

Her guts heaved, turning inside out like a rubber glove. And her hair—always her hair—fell into a curtain of modesty, covering her misery with its satin sheen.

When it was all over, she dropped back to the pillow, panting at the finish line of the race she had run with the devil.

He emptied the mess and flushed it away, coming back with a dampened towel. She draped it over her face as though hiding herself from his cool, surveying eyes. Only her profile, breathing beneath, showed the stubborn signs of life.

"You blasted fool," he said, knowing that she waited his judgment.

"But you were leaving me," Eve muffled weakly from beneath the towel.

"You're damned right," he said without mercy, "And I still am."

"Chuckie..."

The appeal didn't reach him.

Her hand waved like a palm frond, blindly searching for him.

"Give it up," Chuck said. "It's finished. *Kaput.* We've both had it, Eve, so call off your dogs."

"Chuckie..." The appeal again, as though she hadn't heard a single word. "What happened to me? What did I do?"

"Whoever knows the answer to that, baby, wins the golden ring."

"I was dancing in that silly bar, with that silly little fat man and the next thing I knew, you were missing." She pulled the towel from her face now and smoothed away damp strands of hair, revealing tired eyes tarnished with helplessness. "Don't you know what it feels like to be... all alone?"

He watched her folding the towel, a meaningless housewifely gesture of neatness. "That's your story, baby."

"The only time I'm not alone," she said softly, "is when... somebody gets in close enough, almost close enough to..."

"Forget it," he snapped. He took the wet towel from the pillow and tossed it into the bathtub.

"I couldn't stand him. Not from the first moment I saw him in that depressing hospital. But then he started to flirt with me and I thought, he likes me a little. Somebody likes me a little." She wiped her lips with the back of her hand. "Chuckie, if only you could like me... a little... sometimes." Her voice trailed off wistfully.

"No good," he persisted, turning from the sight of her reaching like a begging pup.

"And then we all went out together because it seemed like the gracious thing to do. Then the next moment... Why did you go? Can't you just tell me that? Tell me why, when we were just starting to get human with each other?"

"Look, let's face this, Eve. It's the same damned merry-go-round and I want off. There's no use logging up hours trying to untangle the messed up psychology that makes you you and makes me me. All right?"

"I just can't stand to hear that exasperation in your voice."

Eve lifted herself up onto one elbow. The shoulder of her dress slipped down her arm, revealing the curve of her strapless bra with its overswell of flesh. All the makeup had come off her face. She looked hardly sixteen with her mouth slightly open. A rocky, frightened, lost sixteen. One stockinged foot twitched nervously, the toes digging under an edge of the blue blanket.

It came to Chuck with a wallop that the play he'd started in Robin's pool needed to be finished. The feeling pummeled in his groin, kicking like an embryo pressing to be *birthed.*

He told himself it was the liquor and the aggravation. But he told himself in vain. The iron will that was going to walk him straight out of the room had already begun to melt. He knew he was staring at the moist lips that could suck him into quick sand. Staring and leaning toward her—like a damn fool kid about to reach for his first experience.

Sex was her weapon—for and against her—and she was drawing him into her net like a fisherman claiming his prize. Fingers of desire pushed at the backs of his eyeballs, bugging them sightless. She looked to him like a bursting tropical fruit that he wanted to split open, to feel the trickle of its liquid engulf him stickily.

"I never wanted anybody but you," she mumbled, her lips closing slightly with pain, slightly with the veil of her need. "I'm a no-good rotten bitch. But I belong to you. You're all that makes sense after the ball is over. If you walked out on me, I'd come crawling. Any time of day or night, I'd beg for you." She leaned forward and caught his knee in her hot palm. "Anything you want, Chuck. On any terms."

The hand held fast and he couldn't pull away. He heard the echo of Robin's mockery daring him to make her feel. His blood became the warmed, lighted water of her pool lapping into his dry mouth. And he knew that what Eve said was true. No matter how bad they were for each other, he was the crutch that she hobbled on from one day into the next.

Maybe he could turn and walk out on her. Maybe he could. Maybe there were still good times waiting for him somewhere. Maybe there were still kicks for the living.

But for him? For Eve?

The devil had clapped his hands in glee, knocking their heads together. Sewing them tight into his bag of tricks.

And his good intentions? Maybe they were only doped up dreams like Eve's.

Heavily, he dropped onto the bed, letting the sickened weight of himself fall beside her. A roulette wheel began spinning in his stomach, scuttling the little white wheel of desire round and round, faster and faster, vibrating on speeding ridges. His legs entwined her and drew her body up close.

Willingly, her arms went around his waist. He felt the heels of her palms slide down his back. Her fingers fumbled with the buckle of his trousers.

"Save us," she whispered. "Make us be happy."

Her futile, childish hope lashed him into a fury. His mouth found her tongue and wanted to draw it out by the roots. His arms circled her tightly, his heart beating angrily into the crushed softness of her breasts.

But his violence only whipped her into heights of pleasure. The fragment of her body, like a tattered cloth, fluttered, swaying and slapping, begging him to give and to take.

Desperate, he tormented her, abused her body, releasing the wild, mad seed that grew dark within him.

"Need you . . . need you . . ." Eve whispered.

She was sick and exhausted, yet the tiny fist of her compulsion pounded at him to help her.

He held her, digging his elbows into the yielding mattress, crushing every part of her, driving to quiet her . . . perhaps forever . . . at least for now.

Then he lay hulking and silent, encompassing the smallness of her new found passivity beneath the sprawl of his own sweating muscles. His ribs felt like spikes as pain heaved with every breath.

"It's going to be okay," Chuck said to her searching face.

What else can you say when you're holding deuces?

CHAPTER SEVEN

"I don't want you to get a job," Eve said, smiling virtuously, hands folded over the blankets.

She sat with pillows propped behind and sipped occasionally from the mug of coffee beside her on the bed table. A long tendon extended down the side of her neck. The muscle beneath it twitched now and then as final remnants of the drug dissolved in her body.

Chuck, in a reading chair, nosed his attention at the classified ads of the *Los Angeles Times*. He held it between his face and hers, burying himself once more in the old set of good intentions. He felt only emptiness where the old nugget of resolution used to live, empty as a ghost. But he didn't want Eve to see this. He needed to prevent her from sinking in the hook of her nagging promises that made a tragi-comedy of them both.

"You know you can't stand holding a job," she said. "I don't want you to do anything that isn't right for you, dear."

He rattled the paper, turning a page. "I'm looking at the houses for rent," he said without enthusiasm.

"Oh."

He heard the silence of consternation. "It'll be a good thing," he said before she could start again. "Besides, I need a permanent mailing address."

"Rent a whole house?"

"Why not?"

"Sounds expensive," she said casually.

"Not if we can cut down on the liquor bill. And who knows? Maybe I'll manage to get a book together. Maybe even a series. God knows, I've got enough notes for 'em."

He heard himself sounding domestic and settled. Like a soggy dish towel.

"And what about Bubber?" Eve said. The question was barely audible.

"What about him?" Chuck kept his manner noncommittal. He had blocked Bubber from his mind. Locked him like a traitor on the other side of the gate.

"I don't know," Eve's voice trailed off. "Only..."

"If Bubber wants to find us, he'll find us. But as far as I'm concerned, he's out. About time, anyway, that he got his own wife and his own troubles."

"You sound angry with him, Chuck."

"Just fed up."

"Anything you say..."

"Yeah."

He hadn't slept at all and he needed to get away from her. Looking for a house was as good an excuse as any. Besides, a couple of months in the sun, some regular swimming, maybe he could work off some of the damned depression dragging at him like moss. He checked off a couple of places, then tore out the page, folding it into a back pocket.

"Find something?" she said, snuggling down a bit beneath the covers. "Let me see."

Resignedly, he took the page out again and handed it over. While she looked at it, he pulled on a fresh shirt and ran the electric razor over his chin.

"This one sounds nice," Eve said conversationally.

"Which?"

"The cottage for a hundred seventy-five."

"I thought so, too," he said. She was being agreeable and he felt glad to go along with it. "Guess I'll run over there first."

"Wait," she said, moving down the shoulder strap of her night gown. "I'll come along."

"You stay in bed," Chuck commanded.

"But I want to come with you."

"You couldn't make it to the car," he said bluntly. "Let alone ride around all day in the sun."

"You're going to be out all day?"

He heard the first flicker of suspicion and sighed inwardly. But he wasn't going to give in this time. No more fights. No more chances for tantrums and wild acts of self destruction. Last night was the final dose he intended to take from her.

"I'll only be gone as long as it takes," he said into the mirror.

Eve sighed. He knew she felt his no-nonsense attitude this morning. The question was whether or not she would give in to it.

"If you think it's best," she said in her little-girl voice, half obedient, half slyly fishing to discover what else he intended to do when out of her sight.

"Phone me as soon as you find something?" she said.

"Of course."

Chuck snapped up the paper and strode briskly from the room, almost running from the hovering complications that could trap him with her for the rest of the day.

The blue sky opened wide and relaxing as he hit the sun. An iron fist loosened from around his lungs. His glance followed a group of girls running down the sidewalk in shorts and he knew with dead certainty that whatever he had once felt for Eve was finished.

All that remained was this sickening shell of their life together.

But he still intended to get the house and quit this globe circling like a homing pigeon with amnesia. With or without Eve, he had to shore up his life, steady it into a sensible routine that would leave time for lots of work.

At thirty one, he had done exactly nothing with his life that amounted to anything within a mile of making him glad. He just about knew from one month to the next where the next check was coming from. But there was nothing in the bank. No reserve to count on, no kernel to gamble with on the long-shot of a book.

He turned these thoughts over while the Morris took him along the freeway. And by the time Chuck had reached the place for rent, he had made up his mind to take it without thinking too hard about its conveniences for Eve.

The renting agent threw Chuck a non-stop spiel as he inspected the rooms. He heard the slick words and they made him feel creepy as though he ought to look for the rat holes or the leaks in the roof that the words were supposed to cover.

Actually, it wasn't a bad little house, Chuck saw. It had a view of the hills from almost every window, a neat kitchen with flowered wall paper that Eve would like and a cubby hole of a den where he could set up his work things and forget about his other troubles. The plasterboard ceilings sagged a little and nail heads made a line of yellowish scabs beneath the thin coating of white paint. But sun floated in. The spare furnishings were simple but sturdy enough for an occasional set-to of temper.

He only had to wait until the couple ahead of him decided it wasn't close enough to shopping for the little woman.

Writing a check for the deposit on a two year lease felt like the first good thing that had happened to him since he'd grown his first beard.

They signed the contract at a long log table in the living room.

"Your wife is going to love it here," the agent said. "We don't get a speck of smog this high."

The agent smiled proudly, as though this feat were his personal accomplishment. But Chuck hardly saw the smile as his mind clicked over with the first hint of something familiar. He got up and went to peer again from the double window.

"That's the Drive you're looking at," the agent said helpfully. "Some nice homes up there if you're ever in the market to buy."

Chuck felt for a few coins in his pocket and rubbed them together as he realized what he could see up along the curving of terraces. "I thought this was supposed to be a big, sprawling county," he said mostly to himself. "But I tell you, man, it's smaller here than New York."

Behind him the agent cleared his throat in a gesture of nervous puzzlement. "If you're worried about intrusions, I can assure you ..."

"Nothing," Chuck interrupted. "I like it here just fine."

He waited for the bustling little man to go and leave him alone with his thoughts. It would take some getting used to. But nobody had to know. He wouldn't tell Eve. And he certainly had no intention of going back up to that damned house. Not unless he intended to drown himself in the pool.

Thinking of Eve, he realized that he was supposed to phone her. Yet something couldn't drag itself to the telephone and he sighed with relief when he discovered that it was disconnected.

Finally, alone with the spread of comfortable rooms, the agent far away, Chuck's mind snapped back to practical matters. It came through the fog of complications that his room would be up at two o'clock at the hotel and his typewriter confiscated.

It was just an old Royal portable that rattled but it held the feel of his touch and the rhythm of his sentences. A faithful servant not to be discarded lightly.

He had half an hour to get back there and thoughts of his promise to call Eve disappeared as he aimed for the hotel.

His room smelled of stale smoke and the typewriter sat open on the desk where, in triumph, he had left it.

"Hello, little Minx," he said to it and let himself down into the chair. There was something about his typewriter that smiled, that knew secrets. An oracle in a black case that would give up its mysteries if he would but touch the keys ever so lightly, without really trying.

Chuck rolled in a piece of paper and stared at its blankness that reflected all the unspoken questions.

What can you tell me today that will be of some use? he thought.

He lifted his hands to the keys.

Words clattered out in a burst. For a while, they didn't seem to make any sense. But his fingers, moving automatically it seemed—like the keys on a player piano—kept up the rhythm, the hint of meaning within the lettered melody.

He pulled the third page out and started to crumple them all without reading them through. He prickled with the feeling that something had gotten said that he'd rather not see. For he had learned that in the definiteness of words lay the undeniable vapor of truth.

Go on, you bastard, read it.

He pushed the chair back and let his gaze scan across the type.

And when he finished reading, he knew what he had to do. If it pushed him down the drain forever, one unfinished chapter in his life had to be written.

CHAPTER EIGHT

Chuck locked the typewriter case and lifted the telephone to ask the Operator for Barney or Robin McDermott's number.

A cold film of sweat lay over his back. It felt like the stupidest move he could make, to phone her. Yet he knew he must.

The phone buzzed and buzzed. If nobody were home, maybe he could shrug the impulse off as only a mocking thrust of his subconscious.

But luck wasn't with him.

The receiver clicked off. Her voice said hello as though he had dragged her up, unwilling, from a dark depth of pleasure.

He had her on the line now, but he'd have to play what he said by ear.

"There's some unfinished business between us that needs to be settled," he said, casting around for something sensible. "I mean, if I'm going to keep my promise to your son, I have to be on good terms... at least speaking terms... with his folks."

She didn't hang up on him. That was a start. But she didn't say much either.

"I wish I could see you," he continued. "Someplace neutral like a bar or a restaurant. Bury the hatchet and all that."

It seemed to her that there wasn't even a hatchet to bury. She'd forgotten about the other night. Certainly their private episode wouldn't interfere with any friendship he might want to show Jim. If anything, perhaps she ought to apologize for Barney. "Barney is one of those men who has to leave a stench wherever he goes. Like a calling card."

Chuck said, “Don’t turn me off, Robin. It’s not like we were a couple of teenagers caught necking in the bushes.”

For the first time, she laughed. Then he heard her covering the receiver. Her voice buzzed to somebody but he couldn’t make out the words.

When she came back, she said, “All right. But no hassles this time, please.”

“Not a wrinkle,” Chuck said.

“So come on up here.”

Surprised at her invitation, Chuck thought better than to question it. He knew only a certain lightness in his soul as though a bulb had gone on somewhere.

He was the kind of guy who could hate himself hard but not for very long. Except about his blunder into marrying Eve.

Robin had let him make a fool of himself. But he had vented his feelings. The anticipation he felt now had little to do with evening things between them. Instead, it moved through him with a feeling of cleanness . . . as though he were on some kind of search.

He grinned, called himself a filthy apostle, then swung out of the room, his typewriter firm in his fingers.

It was easy enough to find her house. The car nosed along almost scenting down its own tracks. And his head felt all in order, clean as a school slate in the morning . . . waiting for the message to appear.

He pressed the doorbell and whistled at the sky. It was a great day.

From the huskiness in her voice, Chuck knew that Robin had still been in bed. He supposed that he’d given her enough time to dress.

But when the door opened and it wasn’t Robin but another woman smirking out at him, he tried to tell himself that this was the maid.

In his heart, Chuck knew that no damned maid ever looked like this.

"Hi," she said in a deep voice funneling up from a deep, firmed-up chest. "I'm Robin's friend Lil." She stepped backward into the room and the sweat pants she wore jiggled a little, revealing that this was no woman to wrestle with if you hadn't eaten your Wheaties. "Don't let it shock you," she continued, making bland conversation. "Angelinos are a strange kind of informal bird."

Chuck veered his gaze off the tight red polo shirt to concentrate on the square face with funny round features in it that reminded him of a domino. From skin burned almost black, her white teeth and eyeballs gleamed in the afternoon cast of shadows. As tall as Robin, she seemed twice as thick and her black curly hair bobbed softly in strange feminine contrast.

"Look, Chuck Tatum," she brought him into an alcove of the livingroom and motioned him to a deep wing chair, "we've been reading your stuff for a long time, Robin and me. You've got a nice, neat style of writing."

He sank into the feather cushions, aware that she was trying to be friendly in her blundering, open way. "It's nice not needing introductions," he said, listening with one ear to sounds coming from another room, perhaps a bedroom.

"Robin'll be in in a sec," she said, sensing his thought. Stretching wide, she let her arms fall to rest on either hip. "We put Barney on an early plane and Robin's been trying to catch up on some sleep ever since."

"You sound like part of the family," Chuck said, feeling for an opener, some clue that would tell him that Robin didn't really take her kicks where it now seemed most likely she did.

Lil's laugh resounded like a metal key at the bottom of an empty barrel. "No. Just friends. Old, old friends."

The protective tone told Chuck why Robin had felt safe in asking him up to the house.

"We used to buzz the tracks together, Robin and me. Before she chickened out for the domestic dangle."

Lil wasn't obscene, just earthy. Meant for good times, hard jokes and straight gin. Chuck stretched his legs and crossed them at the ankles, suddenly aware that he had on argyle socks.

"That was fast," Robin said, coming in on them, her hands tightening the belt of a gold terry cloth robe.

"Been telling Chuck my life history," Lil said, doing a single deep-knee bend.

"Did Lil tell you how she took the Women's in the Monte Carlo Rally with a two stroke Saab?"

"And with penalties yet, for one zonked out parking light," Lil added, disdaining modesty.

Chuck watched Robin keenly, measuring the extent of the little game she needed to be playing just now. He understood why she had given him no argument on the phone. He took the scotch with ice that she offered and flashed her the message that Lil's presence didn't con him into believing one damn word about her insinuated sex life.

There was a brand of woman, he'd known some, who found it easier to steer a guy off her tail by pretending to be a lesbian. Women who didn't have the self-confidence to trust themselves in the trial by physical fire. It was a narrow path to hoe and hard on the unsuspecting dykes who ran consort. That Robin should be playing this kind of hollow shell game seemed right in style for her. It fit in with the blooper she'd married and the pathetic kid she'd taken under her wing.

It didn't take Chuck in for a minute. But the big question was Robin. How much was she hiding from the world? And how much from herself?

And the source of her appeal to him came blasting through. It lay in the contrast between her exterior cool with the interior helplessness. He had a thing for lost women.

"Look, Lil," Chuck said, feeling an easy flair rising from the roots of his libido, "you're a healthy chick. Why don't you go take a couple of laps around the pool while I square a few words with your ol' buddy here?"

He felt Robin's body tighten beneath its robe. Lil shot a glance at her, but Robin wasn't looking back to give her the clue.

"Go on," Chuck urged mildly. "You can keep a bead on us through those shiny glass doors."

"You know," Lil said, trying to blast up with matching authority, "this used to be my house. I gave the orders around here."

"Well, who knows, maybe you will again tomorrow." Chuck lifted the palm of one hand, pantomiming a gentle movement of pushing her out.

"There's nothing you've got to say, Chuck," Robin murmured when Lil had gone, "that Lil can't hear. We've got no secrets."

"Yeah, I know," he said. "I used to have a friend, too." He was thinking of Bubber and his tongue seemed to curl as with the taste of lemon.

"Well, what is it you want?" she said curtly, folding the hemline of the robe over one naked knee.

"First of all, to tell you that we're neighbors."

Robin's head quirked up from the rim of her glass. The blue eyes bore into him with disbelief.

"Really. Maybe three quarters of a mile down that way." He pointed to the road curving leftward into the sun. "And secondly, to let you know I've changed my mind about swallowing your conviction that the world will end for you in ice rather than fire." He set down his emptied glass and straightened his body on the cushions getting hot from his own body warmth. "This, I admit, just happened when I met Lil. Believe me, I was all primed to let the matter drop delicately out of sight. But now? Uh uh."

"You're just another male bastard. Which I believe I've already had the pleasure of telling you."

"True."

"Well, don't inconvenience yourself for my sake. Missionaries come a dime a dozen in L.A."

"Robin, listen to me," Chuck said, knowing that Lil hovered just out of earshot, waiting to be called in like a pet watchdog. "It means a lot to me that you straighten your life out."

"Does it?" Robin touched back the wisp of hair that always managed to come lose. "Tell me why?"

"It's a funny, weird thing." His voice rang sincere. "But straightening myself out with Eve seems to depend a lot on what you do. It's like the old trick with boxes inside of other boxes."

"Nonsense."

Chuck jiggled the melting ice cubes and stared at their rounding edges, trying to find the right words that would explain what had been growing gradually into clarity for himself. The charcoal odor of somebody's Sunday barbecue floated in, seasoning the alcoholic atmosphere with a kind of togetherness.

"All right, let's drop it," Chuck said at last. "The more I talk, the more I hear myself sounding like a witness to the coming of Jehovah."

"Everything okay in there?" Lil called, bobbing behind the glass like a chimp drooling for a banana.

Robin waved her away. "I'll be honest with you just this once, Chuck. The only thing your life and mine have in common is the supreme height of garbage piled on top. Beyond that, the resemblance ends. I have no romantic interest in you, to put it mildly. Nor could I ever. And I'm sure your own blonde-headed noose is pulling you in tighter and tighter all the time."

"That may be," Chuck said to mollify her so that Lil would remain in captivity. "But you miss one important point."

Robin wiggled a foot out of its terry cloth slipper and rubbed the naked sole nervously on the carpet's nap. "Which is?"

"The bond I've got with your son."

Chuck had dropped his ace and now he waited.

"That's not fair," she blurted. "Jim is just a kid. You can't use him for your little act. I won't let you."

"And Lil? Who's protecting her from your little act?"

Robin's nervousness revealed that Chuck had finally crept in to tap at the life sap of her being. She pressed hard on a table model Ronson and stared at the wick coming up black and dry.

"Come off it, Robin," Chuck said, folding in the whip. "We can help each other a lot, if you'll only let it happen."

Chuck spoke truth and he counted on Robin being courageous enough to admit this.

She pushed the lighter away from her and it spun on the tiny tiles of the table. "You know, if Jim weren't involved, I'd turn you off cold."

Chuck settled back, letting Robin have her own way now. He had been right in believing that Robin's only real interest in life centered around the boy. Lil, permitted back into the living-room, eyed Chuck with the first tendrils of suspicion. She pulled the laces of her sneakers tighter with a quick, jerking motion, as though not knowing what else to do with herself, how to fit into this conclave of intimacy that did not include herself.

"I guess Barney ought to be calling soon," Lil said tentatively, "to check on Jim."

It was her way of telling Chuck that the coast wasn't as clear as he might think. He heard her go on to say, "He'll be coming in every weekend now, poor guy."

Chuck knew that Barney would hear about his visit today. Lil was going to have to do whatever she could to stumble things. Her way of lashing out blindly, dumbly at the new, unnamed hurt that had entered her life but that she could not quite grasp.

"Barney has a lot of patience," Lil went on, perceiving that neither Robin nor Chuck seemed to respond. "Lots and lots of patience."

Chuck, knowing that Barney had little if any patience at all, smiled to himself at Lil's sarcasm. But he had no room inside of him to feel sorry for Lil. She obviously led a blunt life where all the figures added up to the right answers. In a way, he almost envied this.

"Look, chick," he said to give her an answer and maybe shut her off, "Barney and I are old friends, too. You can give him my regards."

He caught Robin flinging him a look, asking him to be kind. But kindness was a bitter pill on his tongue. Eve choked him with kindness. A little less kindness, a little more honesty all around was the medicine for the disease that ailed him. And Robin, too.

"Now, you two be good," Robin said to both of them at once. "I've got to get some clothes on. Visiting hours start in less than an hour."

When she had gone off, Lil heaved herself with great effort to further conversation. She was still struggling to play the host, Chuck saw, as though this were her last outpost of advantage.

"So what's on your schedule for the next ten years?" Chuck said to help her along.

"I tell you," she began, finding a roll of Life Savers and catching one on the tip of her tongue. "Los Angeles is a dull place for sports. Did you know that?" Her voice tremored hopefully.

"Nope, hadn't noticed," Chuck said, playing with her. He had to keep the lid on her, though it was senseless and only part of the strange, chaotic will to win that fastened its leech into anything at hand.

"Well, sure," Lil laughed hollowly. "Nobody with blood sticks for more than a few weeks at a stretch. Ease up, refuel, and off again. Zoom." She made a sliding motion with her hand. "You sticking around for long?"

"Who knows?"

"Good place to get fat," she continued. "Or for old ladies with bad hearts." She shook her head with serious prognosis. "You're gonna bore yourself silly."

Beneath the chatter, he sensed her growing desperation. How often during the years had Robin come to cry on her shoulder? How many times had words of affection been exchanged between them with Lil always coming out holding the dirty end of the stick? It gave him something to think about, that Robin needed to lean on this big hunk of gruffness.

"Know what you ought to do instead?" Lil burst with a grin.

"What?" Chuck continued to humor her.

"Write an article on me. You could call it something like…" she paused and pushed out her lower lip in thought, "… Woman Whizzer Wows 'Em. How about that?"

"Yeah," Chuck grinned, "how about that?"

"I used to think that maybe someday I ought to sit down and write my autobiography. You could write that, too, if you wanted. By Lil Eames, as told to Chuck Tatum. Betcha it would sell like crazy."

"You know, you might be right," Chuck said half seriously. "Remind me to think it over."

"Don't worry. You'll have plenty of time to think it over. Robin makes an average run of three and a half weeks on her boy friends."

It was Lil's laugh now. Loud and full and satisfied. Chuck let her have the day.

"All ready," Robin said, returning in a blue denim dress that sheathed her supple body. The composure had returned, curtaining her with invisible armor. "Lil minds the store while I'm out," she explained as Chuck opened the door for her.

"Good," he said. "We'll use my car."

Robin opened the door of her own and stood with one toe on the running board. It was a big old Mercedes convertible that shone bottle green from Skinny's polishing.

"This is where we part company," Robin said with a quick conviction.

"Now, now," Chuck put his hand on the door top. "I'm obnoxious and all that, but why take it out on Skinny? Don't you think I'd like to see him? Don't you think he'd like to see me?"

Robin squinted into the lowering sun and raised one white gloved hand to stare at him with decision. "Frankly, I don't think you give a damn about Jim," she said flatly.

"Come on, honey. How can you say that after the other night?"

He watched her blush and knew that her embarrassment had won this round for him. But he didn't push it about the cars and got into the driver's seat of her 220 instead.

CHAPTER NINE

"I suppose that you know Jim is about all I have that makes me feel worthwhile."

Chuck sensed her mood of confession and let her talk on.

"I married Barney because of Jim and that's the honest truth. You know, I saw this kid going wild, falling apart beneath his own nerves, and it seemed that here was my one chance to do some little thing..."

"So you quit the racing racket with Lil and turned into a one woman Boy's Town?"

"One could describe it that way."

"Don't be offended, Robin. I admire your guts. I think if Eve ever told me a kid was coming in to share the household, I'd split wide open at the seams."

"You'd rather not have any?"

He chuckled. "Suppose they take after me?"

Robin smiled, turning her profile from him. "Don't paint it so black. You may be a mean old bastard, but something lurks in that drizzly soul of yours."

"Yeah? How can you tell?"

"No special compliment," she said. "That's my feeling about everybody."

"You know," Chuck said lightly, "it could take persistence to warm up to a woman like you."

"That's what all the men say," Robin answered with suppressed but acid triumph.

They reached the hospital ten minutes early. Robin didn't want to stop in for a drink to kill time, preferring to ease herself into the atmosphere as though gradually knitting herself into shape for the ordeal of looking at Skinny all soaked up with pain killers.

Chuck went through the admitting procedure with the desk nurse, grinning at Robin when the woman assumed he was Mr. McDermott.

Then they waited with the crowd for the elevator, letting the car go up and down twice before getting in.

Upstairs, Chuck remembered not to offer her a cigarette.

When they strolled into the room, they found Skinny lying with the phone on his stomach. Something guilty lingered around his lips. He spotted Chuck and pushed the phone aside. The receiver fell off the bed and swung, grazing the floor.

"Making dates so early in the day?" Chuck bantered, retrieving the phone and setting it beside the polished pitcher of water.

"Didn't expect to see you," Skinny said, obviously disconcerted. "Sure is great... Hi, Mom."

Chuck rankled every time he called her Mom. He wished he could slap the kid awake, pull him out from under the comfortable maternal wing where he hid from his own dormant manliness.

"Were you calling me?" Robin said with mild surprise. "You know I come to see you whenever I'm allowed." She leaned over and kissed him on the forehead. "How does it feel to be Jim today?"

Skinny scratched under one edge of a bandage. "Not too bad," he said, avoiding the first question. "Nuisance lying here, though. Feels like I'm melting away inside this mummy's skin. Where's dad?"

"Your father had to catch a plane this morning," Robin said, trying for casualness.

"Sure," Skinny said slowly, hardly able to hide the disappointment.

Chuck leaned against the windowsill, watching the interplay between them. One of those kid-needs-father bits that was supposed to tear at the heartstrings.

"Look," Chuck interrupted, "I used to be with my old man every damned hour of the day. Doesn't leave a father much time to be a hero. Means you still have an illusion or two left, if you still miss yours. And that's about all the ideals you'll ever have, Skinny. Take it from me."

He hadn't meant to make a speech but the honesty and strength of his feelings had taken Chuck off guard.

Robin looked up at him with thinly disguised interest. Something around the corners of her mouth softened. She turned to Skinny and put her palm to his cheek. "Never looked at it that way, did you, Jim?"

Skinny twisted a little grin onto his pale lips. The tension lightened almost visibly. "You make a lot of sense, Mr. Tatum."

"First names all around," Chuck said. And winking at Robin, "That's how your mother likes it."

"Did they shovel the Volks into the graveyard yet?" Skinny asked, his thoughts free now to switch to the topic dearest to him.

"No," Robin said.

Chuck sensed that Robin hadn't seen it. That she was making this up to ease the kid.

"Maybe there's something we can save," Skinny said.

"Like the door light," Chuck put in. "Or did you modify that right out of the blame car?"

Instinctively, Chuck knew how to strike the right trotting pace with Skinny and he felt that Robin was glad for his presence now. Glad for the lifted gloom, for the semblance of a carefree world that he could let in for Skinny to glimpse.

The hour flew.

"Will you come tomorrow, Chuck?" Skinny said with a press of eagerness as the nurse opened the door to signal the visit's end.

Robin said, "Let's not pin people down, Jim."

"I'll make it," Chuck said. "There's a snorkeling expedition at the quay that I have to cover in the morning. So I might be a little late. But I'll see you."

On this shaft of promised sunshine, he steered Robin from the room.

As they strolled toward the parking lot, Robin said, "I'll have that drink with you now. But let's make it a soda."

One for our side, Chuck thought. At last the mortar was beginning to crack between the bricks of Robin's wall.

"Whatever you say," Chuck answered, going easy with her now, careful not to frighten away the hesitating bird of herself that was beginning to hop in closer to see what could be in it for her. Idly he mused on whether this starved woman had ever known the abandonments of love. He didn't kid himself that she would give in easily. But any toe hold would do to start. Anything that would keep alive his incentive to pull free from Eve, to get himself off the meat hook.

Placidly, they drove down past Laguna Beach, moving beside rolling green hills that seemed to leap steeply up from the ocean.

She took sunglasses and a cotton sun hat from the glove compartment and settled herself to the streaming warm air that whipped around the sides of the windshield.

"I have to admit, Chuck," she said after a while, "that sometimes you amaze me."

"How's that?" he said, keeping his gaze steady on the road beginning to wind itself along the contours of the beach. The big car fit him right. Its mellowed leather seats caressed his back and hips. He felt firm with the road, appreciating the solid balance of springs that took sway and lean with oiled grace.

"Frankly," she said, "I didn't think you had it in you."

"About Skinny?" Chuck smiled loosely and scratched an itch in one rough spot beneath his chin that he had missed in shaving. "Stick around," he said. "There are lots of surprises."

He curved off the road, found a store and brought back a couple of opened Cokes. "Besides," he continued, "you keep forgetting that I like you."

"That's inevitable."

"Is it?" It was Chuck's turn for surprise.

"Of course."

"How's that?"

"Don't make me say it, Chuck. It might depress you." She bubbled soda to the bud of her mouth.

"On second thought, I guess it is," he said, leaning one elbow on the door. "After three years of my darling wife, you are ocean breezes to me."

"Come on, Chuck, that's not how it goes," she said with a trifle of impatience. "You don't like me because I'm so different from Eve."

"No?"

"No, of course not."

"Then why?"

"Because we're so alike."

"You and me?"

"No. Eve and me."

"You're kidding."

"Am I?"

Chuck felt himself beginning to shake a little behind his navel. As though she had zinged in with an unsuspected arrow. One that hit the bull's eye.

"Isn't it so, Chuck? Think about it."

"I'm thinking," he said glumly.

"Of course. Eve hangs on to you for dear life. I cling to Lil."

He felt the compulsion in her driving to entangle their troubles in words. Catch the slippery fish and pull it ashore where she could grasp it at last. He let her talk. Ease the pressure off. Display all her weaknesses.

And while she spoke, he listened, fascinated by the subtle hypnosis of her truth. He had never been much good as a talker himself. In the written word he could find the truth. But if he lied there, nobody could catch him up. Or if he evaded, none would be the wiser. Now Robin, suddenly uncorked, opened up by her first true feeling of confidence in him, was spilling all the stinking fish from the barrel.

"What you said earlier, Chuck, at my place. About helping each other? Well, maybe we can. Stumble along somehow. I'll keep your mind off Eve. You can keep me away from Lil. Perhaps, if we can really try, we can lead each other out of this filthy jungle."

She gave it to him fast and neat. Chuck sat back quietly, watching her reflect and expand the action he had started. While he thought deep inside his head, Robin thought aloud. They traded the ball back and forth.

"You're awfully quiet," she said at last.

"Because I'm agreeing with you."

Robin smiled. One dark eyebrow arched above the smoky frame of her glasses. "Men usually say I emasculate them with so much talk."

"You probably do," he agreed. "With most men. But me? I like a woman who can say right out whatever she's got to say."

"And nothing shocks you or threatens that ever-lovin' maleness?"

He knew she referred to her relationship with Lil. "I've been knocking around too long for that," he grunted. "And besides, if Eve hasn't killed it in me by now, nothing on earth can."

She reached into his shirt pocket for the cigarettes and lit two. "Here," she said, handing him one. "Now take me home before my hostilities start creeping up again."

"Don't be so damned analytical," Chuck said, veering the car around and heading back toward her place where he knew he would have to deal with another phone call from Barney and balance out Lil's reproaches for having been gone all this while.

Besides, Chuck remembered that Eve was expecting to hear from him. The thought withered, stinging him with its reluctance to face her after the progress he had made this lovely afternoon.

"Even with all good intentions," Robin said, as though reading his thoughts, "one can't cut oneself off so abruptly."

Chuck knew she spoke the truth. Her words summed up all the times he had run out on Eve, only to find her again, somehow, like a forgotten cufflink rolling around in an empty drawer.

He pulled up into the driveway and decided to get straight into his own car rather than go through more banter with Lil.

"See you tomorrow?" he said.

"At the hospital."

He watched her stroll into the canopy of shade extending from the roof.

As he drove back toward the motel, he knew he was going back to Eve. But somehow, after today, he was going back to her a little less.

CHAPTER TEN

The motel hadn't blown away or been shattered by an earth tremor or dissolved by a flood.

The sight of it, standing unchanged, peacefully dilapidated in the lengthening shadows of its slanted trees rather surprised Chuck. And inside, Eve would still be Eve, too. Nagging, curious, clinging, demanding, worn out and beautiful.

He felt as though he were walking backward in time as he came up onto the low porch and swung through the creaking screen door.

Eve had stayed in bed all day. One could see the little fits she'd been having in the pulled out blanket, the bunched pillow, the sooty spread of ashes smudged into the sheet. He recalled Robin's words about Eve clinging to him and knew the loss raging through Eve though she herself didn't realize it.

"Success," Chuck said cheerily, hoping to forestall Eve's fury. "We've got a place to bed down in. You're going to like it, honey, a damn sight better than this dump."

Eve hardly heard him. Her yellow eyes had grown deep with the murk of inner thoughts. "Was it a gruelling day?" she said, starting at him slow. "Driving around in all this hot sun? Did you have to see a lot of people and go a lot of far off places?"

Chuck pulled off his jacket and hung it into the closet almost bare of his own clothes and smelling from the faint sachet of hers.

"I'll live," he said.

"Bet you will," Eve answered.

"Well, if you don't want to spend another night here, I suggest you throw yourself into some clothes and let's get moving."

"Maybe I've changed my mind," Eve said.

"About what?" Chuck said patiently. He hadn't expected it to be easy. And he felt prepared for the usual hassle that she must go through, the fight, the assurances of security, the tears. He settled down and waited as though he had bought himself a ticket for a movie.

"About living in California," she said.

He knew his cues. "And what's the matter with California?" he said without interest.

"I think it's too hot."

"We'll get you an air conditioner."

"They're expensive."

"I intend to afford that and lots more. I'm getting down to work, Eve. Good, stiff work. I need to."

"And me? What am I supposed to do while you're . . . working?"

Chuck smiled into the dark closet at his own nasty thought. "Have you ever considered the possibilities of getting yourself a job, honey?" He said this with mock innocence, yet there was a hint of sincerity in the suggestion.

"Are you kidding?" her voice squeaked. "You know what I'm good for."

"That can earn a living, too," he answered, relentlessly pleasant.

Eve rustled the blankets as sign of her ruffled feelings. "You're being cruel," she said.

He heard her begin a soft whimper.

"Now, stop that," he said abruptly. "And get out of that damned bed and dress yourself. It's almost dark and I want to be out of here."

"I've been wanting to be out of here all day," she answered. "But what good did it do me? You said you'd call and here I was, stuck in this filthy place waiting for a phone to ring that never did."

"I'm sorry," he said with a sudden wave of commiseration, "but it wasn't convenient."

"I'll bet it wasn't."

She was building to the crest of her anger, gathering herself securely, foaming within the heave of her white bosom, jabbing viciously at the blanket with both feet.

"Look," he said, opening the soft leather traveling case and dropping in shirts, "why don't you save some of your fight to christen our new place with?" She slipped from the bed and came to stand beside his bending body. The odor of sleep and warmth and perfume fluttered in the folds of her gown. She shook one hip and the material touched his cheek. "Where have you been all day, Chuck?" she said with sudden scientific interest. "You're in an odd mood."

"I told you."

"Everything?"

He grabbed a handful of socks and dumped them in beside the shirts. "How much of everything do you tell me?"

"Then we're even."

He knew she hadn't given it up. He hunched his shoulders tiredly and waited.

"I don't want to live in this stinking town," she blurted. "I hate it here. We have no friends. Nothing."

"Bubber'll find us again," Chuck said. "Never fear."

Eve knelt beside him. She put one hand on either of his cheeks. "Please take me home," she said. "I don't want us to be isolated and miserable. It's not good for our morale."

"Morale?" Chuck leaned back on his heels and let out a laugh. "That's a new one. What are we, in the foreign service or something?"

Eve leaned in close and put her arms around his neck. "I'm afraid."

"Of what?"

"Just afraid, Chuckie."

Eve huddled close and Chuck knew that she was sincere. The primitive instinct to protect home and self was beginning to rise in her against the unknown force that threatened.

"I'm tired of running," Chuck said. "I've rented this house and we're going to live in it."

Her warm breath clouded his neck. He felt sorry for her misery but he knew that they must both face the inevitable. Better to live separately than drown together. After three years of trying to make things work, he knew that at last he was really beginning to pull up stakes.

"Get with it, Eve. We've got some packing to do."

She did not move away from him. Merely shifted her position, making herself smaller, trying to blend the curve of her body to fit into his.

"Let's forget the house," she pleaded. "I didn't really know what it would feel like, being so far away from everything. Only today, when you were gone and I was waiting. You don't know how lonely it felt. Like I had lost my sense of hearing."

"Make up your mind to it," he said evenly. "We've got a two year lease."

"Oh, Chuckie," she moaned.

He saw the first tear rising and spreading across her curling lashes. "But if it gets too lonesome," he added, "you can always catch a plane…"

Her body trembled and stiffened. He could tell that she was searching for a way to fight this new feeling in him. And he was surprising himself, too. For once, she had not lassoed him into her own chaos. He seemed to be standing aside, watching himself pack, watching her trying to dissuade him with the smallness of her being and the hugeness of her dependence.

She kissed his ear.

"Later," he said and shrugged himself free.

She shuddered and moved away from him now, lurking within herself, watching him with bright eyes, biding time till she would find the opening to his own weakness.

"Well... if this is really what you want... if it'll make you happy..." She waited for him to give in.

"It is," Chuck said with firmness.

"Then I have no choice, have I?"

"None."

Amazingly, she pulled herself together bit by bit, drying her eyes with a tissue, touching her lips together to survey the need for makeup. In silence, she let the gown slip to the floor and bent over the bureau to extract bra and panties.

And now it hit him. The urge to reach for her dimpled flesh, to lose himself inside the depths of her darkness, to devastate her with the rushing force gathering in his loins. "Get your damned clothes on," he said and stuck a cigarette in his face.

He caught the flicker of a wicked smile peep with satisfaction through her eyes. She put her palms to her breasts and lifted them, letting her gaze search each slowly, as though directing his gaze to them in turn. She sank her weight onto one leg so that her hip rose, lifting her behind toward him, beckoning with it.

"Are we really in a rush?" she said languidly.

Chuck grunted something, then dove back into the drawer, plunging his hands into the pile of shorts, dumping them, finding his handball gloves, dumping them, too, making a fast job of getting his things packed while he fought off the dizziness pounding along the back of his neck and tightening in his aching throat.

Silently they fought each other, moving as though on the battlefield of a dream.

But eventually, Eve got dressed.

Chuck dragged the valises to the car, hoisted them into the trunk and blessed the heavens that he had succeeded thus far. He felt that he had gone over the hump and what remained now was simply to start rolling downhill, gathering speed till nothing, not even Eve, could stop him.

He went through the necessary motions of checking out, paid up their back bill and handed over the key.

"Will you leave a forwarding address?" the clerk said.

Chuck's first impulse was to say no. But then, because Eve would want it, he hoped that Bubber would try to trace them. And he gave their new address.

Then he settled Eve into her Chrysler and leading the way in his gray Morris, headed into the second round of his fight for freedom.

The door of the shingled house stood almost flush with the rocky earth and he had to fight to get it open. An odor of damp wood, unlived in for many months, assailed them with an attitude that did something less than welcome them warmly. He was seeing the place now through Eve's eyes as he set their bags down on the uneven floor boards. And her eyes were like thick shades that could close out the strongest sun.

"Guess we'd better turn the heat up," he said with forced cheerfulness and hunted out the thermostat hanging in one corner of the dark, square entrance hall.

Eve switched on a light and examined upward at the dirtied curving bowl of a chandelier. "How much did you say we were paying for this?"

"One seventy-five."

"Without utilities?"

"Right."

"Some bargain." With one foot, she began pushing a valise toward the bedroom.

Immediately, he went to the small room behind the kitchen and opened the typewriter on a single drawered table that would serve as his desk. The red painted chair had a wicker seat that creaked when he sat down and jackknifed his knees to bump upward against the table.

"Well, little Minx," he said softly. "Welcome home."

With the door closed, he could almost believe that Eve was on a jet going to Europe rather than making her tour of criticism through the other rooms. He slipped the package of paper out from its spring clip inside the case cover and set it neatly beside the typewriter, patting the paper and the machine alternately, enjoying the expectation of hours spent here producing something useful for a change.

The window faced away from Robin's house. He could see lights going on in other houses, checking off spots of brightness through the foothills.

His door opened suddenly. Eve came up behind him and put her hands on his shoulders, massaging slowly through his shirt.

"It's going to be all right for us, Chuckie," she murmured. "Promise me."

"Yeah," he said. "But only if you get out of that foul habit you have of banging in here."

"You're locking me out?" she said.

"No. Locking myself in. How the hell am I supposed to concentrate, if you bounce in here any time of the day or night you feel like?"

This was the first time he had ever spoken of his annoyance. Perhaps the first time that it had reached up to where he could recognize it.

"I'm beginning not to understand you," Eve said. "But honestly, I'll do anything you say. I don't want to get in your way ... not ever."

"Fine. We'll get along then."

He hoped that she would take the hint and leave now. But she hovered there behind him, waiting. For what, he did not know. Only waiting, as she always waited, for something to crack open, for something to spill out of each of them and mingle once again into the weird poison they shared.

"Are you going to work now?" she said at last.

Chuck sighed. "No, not now."

"Then come with me into the livingroom. It's rather nice in there. Large, anyway. This must have been somebody's retreat once. I think it's rather cozy."

She was trying.

Trying to pull them together again, just as he was trying to get them separated so that they could look at each other, make evaluations based on sense rather than passion.

Yet he didn't hate her. Didn't wish her ill. "Okay," he said, moving up from the chair. "We'll go sit in your livingroom."

They owned few of the small, decorative belongings that can make a strange house feel like home. But Eve had done what she could. Their marriage snapshot stood balanced against an empty vase on top of a walnut cabinet. Her college diploma photostated to wallet size and encased in plastic stood propped to a table radio. She had even brought in the cracked green shell of a cocoanut and filled it with fern, making a bouquet for the log table.

"Nice," Chuck said, looking around.

"Come sit beside me." Invitingly, she patted the studio couch cushion beside her.

Chuck lay down on the foam rubber and put his head on her lap. Her hand reached to fondle his and she stroked the side of his arm quietly.

No words passed between them. Beneath his head, he felt the roundness of her thighs moving slightly apart, making a more comfortable hammock for him. Her free hand fingered to his scalp and began slowly rubbing above his temples.

At moments like this, he felt a wave of the old closeness they once had known. Like a rusty nail jabbing at his ribs, he knew her desire to be good, to be good for him.

"We'll be fine," she whispered, lulling herself. "I just had the jitters for a minute. You know how I am."

Yes, he knew. And the nail seemed to twist in his flesh. He remembered the letters of an ad in the paper that began: What is it worth to you to feel like a man?... And his own maleness began to rise, protective, persistent, needing to fight the battle for freedom not for himself alone, but for Eve as well. No matter what the temptation, he must always realize that they could only be poison for one another. The time for reconciliations was past. Somehow, in some way, he must lead her away from him, away from her own throttling dependence, her addiction to their marriage.

"You do love me, Chuck?" her voice trembled, groping like a little child in the darkness of her confusion.

"Yes, I love you, Eve," he said and it was true.

Her fingers slid now inside his shirt. He felt the cold, frightened seeking of her. It would not help to try to speak sense to Eve. She must find out for herself and be convinced of the futility reigning supreme above their affection.

"Sometimes I don't feel you do," she said with a hope for contradiction in her voice.

Chuck shifted his weight on her lap. He knew he could not reassure her. Could not promise what could no longer be fulfilled.

"I love you," he said, trying to be gentle, "but it's different."

"Different? From what?"

"Just different," he said, not wanting to go too far. If he pushed, she would get angry. The temper would burst again. And they'd wind up tearing at each other, then making love again like wild animals in the night.

"I don't feel different," she pursued. "I feel like I always do when we're together like this."

He kept silence. Let her talk herself out.

"I keep hoping," she said, "that a magic wand will come and wave away all the trouble between us."

"But it never comes, does it?" he said now.

"It will," she sighed. "It must."

"I used to think so, too."

"But you don't anymore?"

Eve's face bent over his and he looked into it upside down. He watched her throat bob as she swallowed, tracing her anxiety down to where she locked it safe in one corner of her chest.

"I'm tired of fighting," he said. "It wastes too much time."

Her palm against his chest warmed itself with his body heat." He sensed the life of her leaning toward him, begging that he release himself to her.

Her lips reached his and grazed lightly, moving to the edge of his mouth.

"Let's not, Eve," he said, swinging his head away. "This isn't the time."

"I want to make us a nice house warming," she breathed against his cheek. "Just the two of us, loving and close. The way we like to be."

"No, Eve."

Feelings inside him rose like hands pushing her away.

"But, Chuck, we've got to work this out. You've got to trust me, don't you know that?"

She had hit upon the crux.

"But what is there to trust by now?" he said gently. "You know we're not going to change."

"We've got to try."

She was begging him. Begging him, it seemed, to forget his clarity, his hold on the truth of things. Her lips found his again. The tip of her tongue moved out, like a little bird, to seek him. He felt himself beginning to respond.

"Please, Eve, you're just making it harder than it has to be."

"I love you."

The old refrain. Over and over. Looking for salvation, proving nothing.

"You're tired," he said. "It's been a rough couple of days. You ought to get some sleep."

"But I don't feel sleepy."

Yes, he knew this. Knew how her anxieties pumped energy nervously.

Insistently, her lips stayed on his. She swung around to hold onto him better, making of their bodies a giving and taking of desire, a feeding trough from opposite ends of one tube.

"If you ever stopped loving me," she murmured, "what would I do?"

"Find somebody else," he answered with mildness. "Somebody who can give you what you need."

Eve grunted as though he had punched her in the stomach. She wiggled around so that they were lying side by side. He felt her rapid breathing flutter behind her breasts. One hip pressed against his waist. A tightened thigh lay atop his leg and the ankle bone pressed into his calf. He pushed her hair away from his face. It covered him with fragrance, blocking out air, smothering sensibility, dazing him with the insistence of her vital presence.

"Kiss me, Chuckie."

Her face, lying flat on the gray sofa, waited. The nostrils of her small nose quivered.

The violet hued evening drew its softening veil over her flesh, taming the nightmare, creating a beauty that expanded relentlessly. The cycle of nature knew nothing of morals, neither cruelty nor kindness. It spread, like new grass growing soft and fresh over dung.

"Kiss me," she murmured again, with eyes closed. The fan of her lashes trembled.

Inside him, a magnetic needle had begun to swing wildly, searching for north and south ... for right and wrong.

And meanwhile, she kept lifting toward him, lifting and ebbing away, drawing him into the tide of her body, beckoning him with surface calm and the promises of deeper pleasures.

He kissed her. Kissed her because he had to. Because life was stronger than logic. Because for three years he had kissed her and believed that this time it would be different.

Yet he knew, as he kissed her now, that this time it wasn't going to be different at all. That they were only spinning the wheel faster. Still, his body edged over hers, covering her soft, curving flesh with his weight, with his will, with his desire to do and have done for once and for all.

Her dress slithered up. Magically, she could always manage to give him access to herself, to open the path of herself… the dead end. He saw her eyes rolling beneath their lids, searching out in their blindness the varicolored pattern of her need.

In love, she could be strong. In passion, she could be sure. Her dry warm body could convince him. And with the yielding to desire, he found simultaneously a wildness and a peace.

He dragged down the bit of nylon that covered her.

"There," she said. "Kiss me…"

His mouth moved to where her hand waited to be brushed aside. A thumping of blood inside his nose drowned all thought. His body against hers felt lean and cold as a metal scabbard. He needed incisiveness, the threshing of chaff from wheat.

He lifted onto his knees, aching and shrieking like a banshee, dashing himself full against the yielding enemy, feeling the soft and dark of her, taking with both hands, with thirsty greed, the spoils of the enemy.

Her little cries charted for him the path of her fulfillment. And the drive of his own guts released in a final, all consuming, rib tearing sprint toward home.

They were quiet then, smoking from a single cigarette, lying sweaty and warm in the darkness that had come over them unobserved.

Chuck's head turned to the window. He saw again the beacons of light that had switched on through the hills. He followed the scattered pearls of light toward one, somewhere there among the foliage.

"We're coming along," she said against his ear. "Do you know that?"

But Chuck was thinking of someone else now and realizing that neither diplomacy nor patience could win the day.

CHAPTER ELEVEN

He slept to rise at dawn before Eve came awake.

Scribbling a note that he had gone to the show, he crept out of the house, pulling the door gently shut. She had slept encircled round him like a frightened vine. Now the fresh damp air released him from his own staleness. He tossed fins and mask and snorkel into the back seat. His trunks felt tight, elastic and good beneath his trousers. He wished that Eve could like the outdoors, could feel how nature healed wounds, gave life again, and always forgave the follies of yesterday.

He released the brake and let the car slide away, starting the motor only after he had gone some distance from the house. It occurred to him that he had made a pot of coffee for Eve and had not bothered to take any for himself. Taking care of Eve was like brushing his teeth, something he did that was necessary but not worth thinking about. He hoped that she would have the sense to go out exploring and find stores to buy things. Keep herself amused.

Traffic at this hour was light. He had left a couple of hours too early, needing to avoid an aftermath of conversation, the saccharine taste of sweetness that she would have offered him. He needed, rather, the salt tang of ocean air, clean vistas of sky and water. Simplicity.

At the beach, he pulled off shoes and socks and trousers, leaving on only the knit shirt over his trunks, and strolled down among the gray-white birds, scattered like random pebbles along the curving line of glistening wet sand. They skimmed and ran off, mewling, squawking at his violation of their privacy. A fishy odor hung heavy in the cool air. He flopped down among broken bits of shell and leaned back on his elbows, feeling at one with the wide desolation.

He propped his head on the hard rubber of his fins and closed his eyes, inviting sleep to the sound of water lapping against the solid, wooden legs of the long pier.

Hours later, he came awake to the eye of a hot sun, staring down at him.

The mewling of birds had turned into the piping of human voices in playful groups.

Something behind him kicked sand at his neck.

He turned to look up.

"So Tonto has returned," Chuck said drily. He grabbed for Bubber's ankle and slipped him down to the sand.

"We got work today, Chuck. In fifteen minutes."

"Don't pussy foot, friend. I don't hold grudges. In fact, I'm kinda glad you didn't chicken out all the way."

Bubber unbuttoned his flowered shirt and rubbed sun tan oil on the hairy mound of his belly.

"Not talking?" Chuck said.

Bubber unwrapped a sandwich and bit into it. "It's your move."

"Forget it."

Bubber's mouth worked lumps of food from one cheek into the other. "That's not like you, man."

"I said forget it."

Bubber shook his head slowly. "We gotta clear the air first."

"Okay," Chuck said relentlessly. "Start."

"You're playing with me, Chuck."

"Sure I am." He kept looking at Bubber and thinking of Lil. The resemblance between them made him want to laugh in some kind of twisted way. "Come on," he said abruptly. "Let's get to work."

They moved toward the quay, walking along the water's edge where the sand packed hard.

"Come on, Chuck, blow up at me and get it over with."

"Tell you a secret," Chuck said. "Eve is really pining her heart out for you."

He watched the pleasure dash up against the rocks of Bubber's eyes. Chuck felt a cold thrill go through him as he realized how stupid he'd been all these years, not seeing that Bubber's attachment to Eve was anything but platonic. It had taken Lil to open his eyes. Lil, the good, old faithful friend. And now, seeing clearly, he suddenly knew how to proceed.

"There they are," Bubber said, his flabby chin motioning to a knot of teen-agers clustered beside the pier.

Lean, tanned youngsters gathered with their equipment. Some sat pulling on fins, others did last minute breathing exercises, all seemed excited for the hunt.

"Hi, fellas," Bubber said and introduced himself and Chuck to those whom they did not know.

"You guys gonna do an article about us?" Ted Slats asked, his red crew cut glinting in the sun.

"That's about it," Chuck said. "Mind if we join you?"

"Course not. The Sea Cresters can use any kind of publicity they can get. Good for membership."

Chuck nodded. He saw those healthy kids in contrast to Skinny and wondered if the boy could ever make the grade. He breathed on his mask, then slipped it over his head, feeling the tightness on his skin. The taste of rubber from the snorkel filling in the contour between lips and teeth seemed to cut off all contact with the sociable world. Like birds that could not fly, he watched the boys walking backwards, clumsily on their fins, and joined them at the water's edge.

The shock of cold blasted all thoughts and he sank to half a dozen inches beneath the surface, breathing easily through the tube and adjusting his vision to the watery vagueness, the dimming light. Chuck moved his legs in a slow ambulation, saving wind, following the waving turbulence of Ted Slats, president of the Sea Cresters and a powerful swimmer. He felt the rhythm of his own lungs too shallow, too labored and knew that the life he followed with Eve was not conducive to sport the next day. But the thickness and condition of his muscles still gave him an edge over the boy and he followed with enough ease to the rocks where abalone clung.

Chuck had come to watch rather than participate. As a writer, he lived half in the center of things, half on the sidelines, making a tightrope balance between the two.

Ted loosened a cork handled knife from his waist and grabbed hold of the rock with gloved hands, easing the multicolored abalone shell from its hold. He turned then to Chuck and grinned through his mask, offering the shell for underwater inspection.

The green tinged water, nervous with darting life, demanded bubbles and more bubbles from their snorkels. They rose slowly together, surfacing with a splash. Others surfaced and dove around them like human porpoises, grinning with the delight of physicality, of searching out secrets and worlds unknown to others who merely floated topside in the languid world of warming sun.

"That's a big one," Chuck said.

"We've done better," Ted answered, his freckles crinkling around the edges of his mask.

Ted stashed the abalone in a mesh bag fastened to one of the poles and replacing the snorkel, dove again.

Chuck liked the boy's style, the trim way he handled his tools, the conservative approach to swimming, the solid developing muscle. A good sport. A winner. His type of kid.

They went deeper now, trimming among the logged flotsam of garbage that strollers from the amusement park had tossed over, moving among the dark green and tan spongy growths swaying, the tentacles of sea grass stroking rhythmically at the water, the tight closed shells half hidden in lollops of sand.

He had to remember all of it, the feeling of alienation from life upstairs, the connection between fish who had not made the evolution to land and humans who carried their watery atmosphere encased in their own skins. Catching sight of Bubber around another rock, Chuck wondered vaguely if it had been worth it, the human migration into the dangerous frontier of solid air. Had it been worth it to learn to walk upright... to discover fire... to look at the stars and realize space as yet unconquered? Were the fish and the shells and the mammals who still inhabited the sea not better off? Was the finding of Eve worth the effort, the sacrifice of crawling painfully onto land to stretch and yearn for a hostile consciousness of self, of the universe?

Ted made a sign beneath water and they headed now for shore again, Chuck watching the crew-cut sway a little as it pulled through the pressures and friction of water.

With his mask off, the underwater thoughts fled.

"You've got a great gang," Chuck said. "Good swimmers."

"We play it safe," Ted answered. "Buddy system all the way. No going out of bounds."

"Running a club takes method," Chuck said.

"Sure does," Ted agreed, lowering himself to a towel and stretching out now to catch his breath.

Chuck sat down beside him. "Go to school around here?"

"Getting out this year," Ted said with a laugh. "Finally." He wiped a trickle of water from his nose. "Then it's aqua lungs and diving for money, if I can make the grade."

Chuck nodded to himself. He mused on whether a boy like Ted could have patience with a kid like Skinny.

But Skinny wouldn't be up to swimming for a long time. He decided, with sudden pessimism, that the two would have nothing in common. But still... "How're your grades?" Chuck tried.

"Okay, I guess."

"Math, too?" he said, knowing that was Skinny's strong point.

"We don't talk about Math," Ted smiled. "That's the ogre in the sack."

Information to file.

Bubber came out from the water now, heaving himself up like a grampus. He sat himself into the sand in front of Ted and Chuck. "You're the big boss around here?" Bubber said.

"No bosses," Ted answered.

"I've just about covered this interview," Chuck said, warning Bubber off. Bubber, like Lil, did not quite have the feel for getting the best out of all people.

"Fine," Bubber said with relief. He knew his own weakness.

There seemed nothing more to add and Chuck needed time to get dressed to make it to the hospital.

"You do the first draft," he said to Bubber, "and drop it off at the house." He told him the new address and saying so long to Ted, strolled away.

Arranging his things in the back seat, Chuck felt that the machine was slowly gathering speed. Bubber would do the work as directed. Then bring it out to the house, which would give him a chance for a reunion with Eve.

Chuck hoped that they would have a nice, cozy chat. Maybe curse him out behind his back. He smiled at the picture of Eve resting her little head on Bubber's meaty shoulder. He considered the image of Bubber being sweet and gentle. Something like a trained hippo came to mind ... but just what the doctor ordered.

CHAPTER TWELVE

Skinny waited for him, sitting up now, some of the bandages removed, his yellow complexion not quite so sallow.

"You look ready to get out of this place," Chuck said.

Instantly he knew that Robin had not yet arrived. Skinny's untidy batch of magazines lay as he'd left them, scattered over the bed clothes, half hanging from the table.

"I am," Skinny said. "If they'd only let me. I've been thinking about the Volks and what you said, Chuck. You know, putting a machine together right instead of for the glory."

"Did I say that?"

Skinny laughed. "Don't you remember?"

"Maybe I wasn't listening," Chuck bantered, sorting through the many possibilities that could be keeping Robin. She wasn't the kind to be late for anything. Certainly not for visiting hours to her precious little boy.

"Say, how's your math?" Chuck said abruptly.

"Good enough. But I don't guess I sort it from mechanics."

"You don't have to. You're a senior, aren't you?"

"Sure. Why? Are they going to send me homework? I'm getting out of this joint next Wednesday."

"Good for you," Chuck said, pulling up a chair and straddling it backwards. He could feel the pitch winding up hard and fast. It was only a matter of waiting now for Robin to bat the ball.

The phone began to ring.

Reluctantly, Skinny's hand moved to the receiver. "Yeah... That's okay, Mom. Of course I don't mind... He's here now."

Chuck saw Skinny reach the phone across to him.

Robin's voice was low, too low to be as calm as she was pretending. He listened to the string of her excuses, knowing that he couldn't dare believe a one of them. If she wasn't going to get here at all today, he knew that she must have both legs chopped off or something equally drastic. But he didn't want to argue with her in front of Skinny.

As he cradled the receiver, Chuck knew that he would have to go to the house after he left Skinny. He hadn't told Robin he'd be over. He wanted to simply burst in on her, catch her in the middle of whatever it was. See the truth in its own nakedness. Catch it and hang on and defeat it before it could escape again into the shadows that Robin nurtured.

But for the next half hour he had to be casual. Yet he sensed that his own concern had not carried over to Skinny at all. If anything, he saw that the boy was glad for this opportunity. Glad that his mother hadn't come for once.

It was a theme that Chuck wanted to pursue.

"Too bad she couldn't make it," Chuck said casually.

"She'll be here tomorrow. Don't worry." He seemed uncomfortable, as though itching inside his bandages and anxious to get off the topic.

"You know," Chuck said, feeling dampness between his toes that he had left in his hurry to get here, "my mother died when I was seven."

"Well, mine died when I was born. What does that make me?"

The challenge, unexpected, fiery in Skinny's voice, startled Chuck. Startled in a way that pleased him and he realized that somewhere in Skinny there was still some backbone.

"I got the feeling that you and Robin kind of liked each other."

"I like her fine," Skinny said, pushing a magazine from his bed onto the floor. "She knows a lot that most women don't."

"So what's the beef, kid?"

Skinny's eyes appraised him. Chuck sat still for it, letting it ring through that his own feelings were sympathetic, but also fair to Robin.

"Who says I got a beef?" Skinny answered.

"It's plastered all over your face."

"Well..."

Chuck heard the tone of evasion, but he had to have this out with Skinny. It could mean a lot to his future... his future with Robin. "She hangs on your neck too much. Tries to make a kid out of you. Is that it?"

"Sort of."

"Come on," Chuck insisted. "I've been square with you."

He saw Skinny swallow the challenge. "Well, the truth is... Her and my Dad. They don't exactly like each other any more and I'm supposed to choose sides. Well, I can't," Skinny blurted. "I can't hate my own damned father, can I?"

His loud, squeaky voice told Chuck the whole story and he let it ride. There was no point in cutting Skinny to ribbons. It simply remained to make Robin see that her efforts with the kid were not all the chapters to make for a happy ending. If Robin could give up her stranglehold on the boy, if she could just relax a little and begin to live for herself...

He left Skinny twenty minutes later, figuring out how he was supposed to get the boy's feelings across to Robin without destroying her in the process.

It was going to be a dangerous game. But it was the only way.

He shot the car through traffic and back to Robin's house, his mind distracted by this problem which yielded no solution. The stew seemed to be thickening with bits and pieces added as he went along. And yet Robin's troubles, their complexity, were drawing out and exercising his own strengths.

He pulled up in front of Robin's place feeling both sad for her and glad that at last he dare hope to draw her irrevocably from Barney's clutches. For without her attachment to the boy, there could be no point to her remaining with Barney.

His mind sorted opening sentences while he rang the bell.

But when Robin came to the door, they blew away to dust.

She didn't have to explain why she hadn't come to the hospital. It was written all over her face. Spelled out in one puffed eye and a split lip that swelled the left side of her face into a grotesque grin.

"Oh," Robin said in a little explosion of surprise. Her hand shot up to cover her face.

"Don't bother," he said, stepping inside. "I already caught the show."

She came in behind him, keeping like a wounded thing to the walls of the room. "You didn't tell me you were coming."

"That's the idea," he said, not looking at her, not wanting her to feel ashamed.

"If I'd known …"

"You would have pretended to be out. I know you by now, my friend."

"Yes," she said softly, "I guess you do."

"Then who did you expect was at the door?" he said, filling a glass from one of the decanters on an open cabinet shelf. "Lil?"

Robin's silence was the answer.

"Lil coming to apologize?" he continued. "For having lost her poor little temper?" He jiggled the ice cubes and let them fall to his mouth, needing the cold of them without the liquor, needing something to shock him back into anger from this whirlpool of pity that was surrounding him.

"It's no good, Chuck," Robin said quietly.

"What's no good?"

"This poor little fight I'm putting up. I feel like a kid kicking up sand."

"Well, you ought to feel like a prize fool," he said, getting hold of his feelings and steering them to where they would do the most good. "Now, not even my little Eve would stand up for a hassle like that." He jerked one thumb over his shoulder to point it at her face where she stood behind him.

"Chuck, why don't you drop it and get out?"

It wasn't a question. It wasn't a statement. Just a voice on the wind.

"Is that what you'd like?"

"Frankly," her words were smudged by the swollen lip, "I don't know what I want anymore."

"And what about your lovely, adoptive son?"

He heard Robin draw a breath. "What is that crack supposed to mean?"

"Isn't all this worth it for him?" he said cruelly.

"Sarcasm doesn't become you, Chuck," she said. Her loafers clicked leather soles and heels around the wooden border of the room as she went to pull the glass doors closed against the upstart of a breeze. "You know how I feel about Jim."

"Yes," Chuck said. "And I know a lot more than that."

"So we're all demented. Do something," she said with great acidity. "But stop all this talk talk talk for nothing. I can go in circles by myself without your help."

"Robin," Chuck said impulsively, "you know that Jim needs buddies and self-respect just like any other fellow growing into manhood. Why don't you come away with me and let the kid find himself?"

"You're out of your mind. Jim needs me and he means more to me than you ever will, Chuck. Believe that."

It was a stab and he let it go through him, disconcerted by screeching brakes of another car pulling up close to the house.

"That's Lil now," Robin said. "I wish you'd go."

"I'm staying."

"At your own risk."

Chuck leaned one shoulder against the wall, bracing himself for the anticipated bluster that could be Lil's only reaction to finding the live obstacle of Chuck standing in the way of her reconciliation with Robin.

He watched Robin go to the door, the tails of her little boy shirt swinging with the movement of her behind.

"Got here as fast as I could."

Chuck heard Lil's breathless and innocent voice. He knew suddenly that he had jumped to all the wrong conclusions and stood now in the center of a fire he could not have predicted.

Lil's footsteps thundered into the room. She steamed straight for Chuck, moving with head down, rhinoceros like, reminding him comically of Bubber as Bubber had reminded him of Lil.

It felt funny, but he saw that it was really pretty grim. Her thick fists turned white at their knuckles as they lifted into the air.

"Whoa, there," Chuck said, trying to veer her off. "Hold it, chick."

Deaf and blind with her rage, she steam engined in. A fist shot toward him with the speed of a piston.

Chuck ducked and got caught in the groin with one rising knee. Breath huffed out of him.

"Lil, no," Robin called but Lil heard nothing.

She lifted her fists and started to bring them down like hammers.

Chuck knew that this was no screaming little lady. His eyes still bugged out from the kick. In selfprotection, his hands shot out and caught her wrists. With a judo pull, she twisted free and cut him across the side of his neck.

"You bitch," he yelled. "Lay off."

Her face, despite its sunburn, seemed drained of blood. Her eyes, glassy and blank, seemed to be staring at a vision of insane destruction. Chuck had slapped women in his time when they needed it. He wouldn't hesitate to take this one down. Only she wasn't fighting him as a woman. She demanded with the weight and death-wish of her that he fight her man to man. And this he couldn't do, knowing that despite her strength, despite her rage, he could smear her out on the walls.

But he sailed into her, thinking to pin her to the floor and keep her there until the fury played itself out. His arms grappled round her thick waist. His head went into her belly. Together they plummeted to the floor. He felt one shoulder smack into the carpet and shovelled himself over to sit on top of her.

Robin, running, fell to her knees and bent over Lil yelling at her to give it up.

But Lil's face shook and quavered. She shut her eyes tight against the indignity of Chuck on top of her. Her fists punched low against his back. Her knees came up, trying to lever off his weight.

"Stop it. Stop it," Robin shrieked, banging the floor beside Lil with her fist.

Lil shuddered and gathered herself for one final effort, heaving with a great squeal of breath to arch the steel band of her back.

Chuck curved over her and held fast. The solid one ninety of his six two physique kept her anchored securely.

Realizing her defeat at last, Lil's face twisted into a grimace and she broke into dry sobs of disgrace.

Instantly, Chuck lifted off her and sailed away to a distant bedroom, to leave Lil in peace with the shattered bits of her self image.

He didn't even want to hear the conversation. Robin's soothing voice followed him and he banged the door shut. Twice in one week, he had come on like a bulldozer. First to Bubber. Now to Lil. It wouldn't have surprised him to find a quarantine sign pinned to the back of his shirt.

He sat down on the bed and lit a cigarette, watching the match trembling in his fingers. He smoked in silence, hoping that Robin could get the pieces back together and send Lil on her way. A buzz of voices filtered through the door and he resigned himself to being self-exiled for maybe an hour.

A smell of fresh after-shave lotion tweaked at his nostrils. It detoured the course of his thoughts and he looked up to the top of the chest of drawers. A bottle of Mennen Skin Bracer stood open on a doily. He got up and fingered the cap lying at its side.

Slowly, curiously, he rolled the cover between thumb and forefinger. Lil might want to think of herself as a man but he knew for damn sure that she didn't shave. He hadn't smelled this on her anyway.

And Skinny wasn't home to use it.

The nut cracked wide open and Chuck saw the meat . . . Barney's brain . . . lying discovered in the palm of his hand.

So Barney hadn't gone back to New York after all.

Chuck whistled softly to himself.

The question was, Did Robin know or did she not know that Barney hadn't gotten on the plane?

And other questions grew out of this one.

Was Robin responsible for all this mess? Had she been holding out on him?

And if so, why?

Why?

CHAPTER THIRTEEN

He hung on until Lil's car rocketed out of the driveway.

But he didn't have to go looking for Robin. She came in to face him.

"I know what you're thinking," she said, taking the initiative.

"So what's the answer?"

He put the cover into her palm and stood back, thrusting his hands into his pockets, shovelling coins around.

Carefully, she screwed the cap back on and took the bottle into the bathroom to set it on a shelf in the medicine cabinet.

"I don't know," she said.

For the first time, he wondered if he could believe her or if, like Eve, she told the story most convenient for the circumstance, forcing herself to accept it as the truth.

"Well, when did you find out?" he said, hoping to catch some thread that would reveal her to him.

Robin came back into the room, rolling one shirt sleeve neatly above her elbow. Lil's tears stained the front of it, making ovals of dampness that clung to the bra straps beneath.

"Last night," she said. "He just walked in on me saying that he couldn't keep his mind on the job with Jim in the hospital."

"Okay. Then what?"

Robin shrugged. She sat down on the bed with one foot beneath her thigh. The knot of her hair had come undone. It fell loosely over her back. Chuck realized that this was the first time he had seen her really looking soft.

"Then nothing. As usual. He kept giving me his talk about how we ought to get together for the boy's sake. And I kept reminding him of how impossible that would be."

Chuck thought back to his own situation the night before, going cold with the strange parallel of circumstances that echoed himself in Robin and Robin in him.

"So he stayed over," Chuck urged, needing to hear it out.

Robin nodded. "He stayed over but he wouldn't go to sleep. He kept getting angrier and angrier. Sorrier and sorrier for himself that he had, in all innocence, married such a cold fish." She managed a little smile. "You've never heard Barney being innocent. It could make an elephant retch."

Chuck handed her a cigarette.

"Well," she continued, "the sorrier he felt for himself, the more certain he became that I had to melt in panting thrills to his love making." Her lips tightened now. "So I did," she said flatly. "I let him. This was the first time in over a year and I think he must have forgotten all those other times. So he kept trying and trying till he knocked himself out. Only he couldn't help noticing that I might just as well have been reading the encyclopedia for all the good it did me."

Chuck pushed an ashtray across the quilt and watched her shave off the curving cylinder of an ash.

"Well," she went on, "you know what that can do to a man. Especially a lady killer like Barney. He couldn't stand the sight of me all cool and in order when he had crumpled over. From there on in it was the usual routine. You see it in the movies... the adult movies, anyway. All temper and frustration breaking out over hell. And here I am..." She lifted her hands and managed a weak smile. "... calling Lil to cuddle me as usual and finding you at the door instead." She let herself fall back to the pillow. "I guess that's life."

"And you stand still and take it," Chuck said.

"Yes, that's exactly what I'm doing until something better comes to mind."

Chuck took the stub of her cigarette away and lowered the ash tray to the floor.

"Listen, Robin, can I tell you something?"

"Why not. I've got big tin ears."

"You're not going to like it, but I think you ought to know..."

Because she was running straight into the flames, because nobody stood to gain anything from her sacrifices of self, Chuck squared with her about Skinny's true feelings. He tried to do it easily, gradually. Tried to drain the hurt for her out of his telling. But he told it all, needing to make her understand that Skinny did not need her or want her, that there was no reason for her to remain the victim of Barney's brutality.

She listened quietly, staring up at the blue wall paper designed in little stars and crescents. Without flinching, she heard him out, wetting her lips now and then as though to steady something inside her. She didn't even ask questions. Nor did she try to contradict.

For Chuck's voice came across with conviction. And mingled in it was the flavor of sportsmanship that he knew she could understand.

You play the game and you play it hard. If you win, you don't go wild with triumph. And if you lose, you don't sink into the ground with gloom. You play the game for the game's sake and shake hands when it's over. Tomorrow is another day, another match.

Chuck softened all his words to this aura and waited when he had finished for Robin to take Skinny's attitude constructively and in good faith.

For a long while she was silent. Then she got off the bed, went to the livingroom and poured drinks.

Chuck waited for her, knowing that she must be alone for a while, as Lil had needed to be alone.

When she returned, she handed him a glass and sipped quietly from her own. Only a faint smudge on her cheek told Chuck of her fight to conquer the wave of hopelessness that his words had brought her.

"I can say one thing for you, Chuck." Robin rolled her glass between her palms. Her face seemed almost as pale as Skinny's. "You don't leave a woman with any illusions."

Chuck snorted. "Why do women always want illusions? What the hell is the matter with reality once in a while?" Filled with vehemence, he squinted out the window, needing room for the energy inside him to expand slowly so that it wouldn't explode. Right now she needed tenderness and quiet. A chance to recoup. But there were other demands that could not wait either. "I hate to bring this up again," he said as gently as possible, "but what about Barney now? Are you going to sit here and mourn over your misplaced maternal instinct or are we going to do something definite for a change?"

Briskness had again crept into his manner. If he sympathized too closely, it might encourage Robin to feel sorry for herself. And self-pity led to inaction. They both needed action now.

"What would you have me do?" she said with a voice that seemed to stare curiously at his businesslike approach.

"Move out of here," he said, listing facts. "Start proceedings for a divorce. I think it's all rather obvious, don't you?"

Now it was Robin's turn to laugh. Her swollen lip spread painfully as she smiled at him. "And drift silently into the night?" she said.

Her mockery told him that it was no good. That his method was more a game with puppets than a realistic dealing with the vagaries and cross purposes of human nature.

"You think about it," he said nevertheless.

"And you?"

"What about me? I've got the daily grind to cope with just now. That little matter of earning a living. I hate to be practical at a time like this, but if I get lost in this thing with you now, I won't be any good to help either of us."

Robin nodded. "You have a happy faculty for putting out fires with the cold facts of day," she said. "So go back home and do your article. I'm just going to sit here and knit up the ravelled sleeve of my soul," she said, the light of humor flicking on again in her eyes.

"That's my girl," Chuck said.

He went to kiss her lightly on the forehead and felt her holding herself quite rigid, fighting her natural instinct to draw away.

"I'll call you later," he said.

"Don't worry about me, Chuck," she said lightly. "I bounce."

CHAPTER FOURTEEN

Chuck left, bathed with the clean feeling that he had done his best. Yet he couldn't be sure that it would work. Supposing Robin couldn't stand up to the truth?

If not, she must disintegrate. Go down the drain like Eve. But in Robin's case, she'd be destroying a young boy's life along with her own. He counted on the fact that she could recognize this. That the conviction of doing something for Skinny's benefit would give her the necessary courage.

He drove past his own house and continued into the valley, looking for a place to get some eggs and sandwich makings in case Eve hadn't rallied to the cause.

As he put the bags into the car, Chuck realized that he had begun to think of his wife as a sick child rather than an enemy to life and loving. The feeling surprised him, yet he knew that this had been growing on him during the past week. It was part of his gradual alienation and drew from him pity and patience rather than the old churning anger.

It was almost five. He sensed time and felt the closing in of premonitions. Hunches, for some people, led to wins at the track. But his own were always bobbing channel markers indicating the possibility of danger.

He shrugged off the supposition that Barney would create more violence. And Lil? What would she be capable of, now that he had inadvertently broken her? It was a nasty business, trampling with cleated shoes on other people's dreams. He needed a pitchfork and the smell of sulphur exuding to warn people away.

Carrying packages in both arms, he pushed the door open with an elbow. "Eve," he called. "Here comes supper."

He heard papers rustling in the livingroom.

Setting the bundles on the telephone table in the hall, Chuck leaned in through the doorway.

"That was quick," he said in a clipped but amused voice. The sight of Bubber hastily gathering yellow pages and pretending to be reading them made a ludicrous picture of a trained bear mixing up signals.

Bubber, having accomplished his effect, laid them down again and crossed his legs with an effort at a casual attitude. "Routine writing," he said. "You'll have to do the rest."

"Where's Eve?"

The question seemed to disconcert Bubber. He smoothed back the thinning hairs along his skull, then didn't seem to know what to do with his hands.

"Eve?" Bubber said.

"Yes, Eve. You remember her."

Bubber swallowed.

"Well, what the hell are you making such a production about?" Chuck said, half laughing, half demanding. "Did she skip out on a plane to Puerto Rico?"

"She's in the . . . she's getting dressed," Bubber answered at last.

The implication of Bubber's statement plus his confusion echoed back to the hassle with Lil. He expected Bubber to accuse him of maltreatment, of the proverbial mental cruelty. He even waited to find himself launched into another fight.

"I trust you two had a happy reunion," Chuck said and left Bubber, going to put the things into the refrigerator.

"Now listen, man," Bubber said, pursuing him into the kitchen. "I never wanted to see you two on the rocks, hear? But that's your story now and you're stuck with it."

"So?"

"So I'm pulling out," Bubber swallowed. "And taking Eve with me this time. Okay?"

Chuck smiled sourly to himself, knowing that Bubber couldn't get from here to San Diego before Eve had spent his last bucks and deserted for greener pastures. "Okay," Chuck said.

When Eve came into the kitchen, Chuck saw that her usual state of chaos was temporarily assuaged. Her yellow eyes shone placid as moons and she was dressed neatly, simply in a cotton shirtwaist that flared comfortably from her hips. Apparently, she had leaned on Bubber's shoulder and been consoled. She had asked for strength and been promised his manly devotion.

Chuck's pity expanded as he saw her. He knew that her calmness was a blind alley. That her own bomb was ticking quietly away in some hidden corner, waiting for its moment.

"Hello, Chuck," she said and her voice seemed, in turn, to be pitying him.

"I understand," Chuck said easily, "that I've walked in on a final curtain?"

He watched Bubber and Eve exchange glances, playing their child's game of hide and seek as though he were blind.

"I'm sorry," she said, folding an empty paper bag and setting it on the shelf above a narrow broom closet. "But it hasn't been working out between us. You said so yourself, Chuck. I've come to believe that you'd be better off without me."

Her manner was all sad wisdom and Chuck did not want to insult her by laughing in her face.

"If that's how you feel about it," he said, taking two eggs and breaking them into a bowl.

"Yes, it's time for us to be sensible," she continued as though disappointed that he wasn't arguing.

Bubber lingered at the doorframe. The hulk of him seemed uncertain whether to come in and be part of this or step discreetly out until Eve called. He swayed back and forth like garbage on water.

"So what are your plans?" Chuck said to ease her gently back into thoughts of departure.

"Merely to leave," she said, watching him wield the fork as he stirred eggs. "Go someplace where it's quiet. Straighten things out. Maybe get a job."

Chuck wondered how she could believe her own foolishness. But maybe... Maybe he was being too pessimistic. Maybe Bubber would, after all, serve sufficiently as her fall guy. He could only hope.

"I wish you the best," he said sincerely.

They both watched him pour the eggs and scramble them in the pan, as though he were performing some miraculous feat.

"Then it's settled," Eve concluded, yet her voice seemed to dangle, still waiting for his opposition.

"Settled," he repeated blandly.

Chuck caught the image of himself being objective and too debonair for the circumstances. It was expected that he put up some fight, something for Eve to push against, something to make Bubber feel justified in his role as the gallant knight.

But instead, he could only try to urge them on.

In silence, he filled a pot with water and set it to boil, slipped a slice of bread into the toaster, put the box of sugar cubes on the table.

"You're one man who can take care of himself," Eve said, still searching for some opener to argument.

"Thank you."

"Well," Bubber's voice intruded, "maybe we ought to get started, Eve."

She flicked him a quick, impatient glance, revealing to Chuck that Bubber was walking in quicksand.

"He's right," Chuck said hastily. "Let's not drag this out."

He saw Eve's brows come together for a moment with hurt and disappointment. But she rallied quickly.

"I've decided to leave tonight," she said, hanging on now to her goaded annoyance.

"Are you packed?" Chuck said conversationally.

"You never gave me a chance to unpack," she said.

Chuck smiled openly now. It was true. "Well, be good," he said. "Take care of yourself."

Helpless as an opened flower waiting for the sun, her face turned to him. "I'll write," she said. "I'll keep in touch."

No doubt, Chuck thought, but he didn't answer.

He stayed in the kitchen with his supper things neatly set before him on the formica tabletop while Bubber carried Eve's bag outside and started the motor of her car.

Alone now with Chuck, Eve seemed not quite so sure of herself. She filled a glass of water and set it down beside his silverware.

"Kiss goodbye?" she said.

He lifted his face and kissed her on the neck.

"Good luck," he said, carefully keeping her access to him shut.

"Good luck to you, Chuck."

He almost held his breath till she was out the door.

Toast crumbled against his teeth as the big car rolled away. He listened to the sound of its motor growing faint and finally blending in with other signs of the coming night.

Maybe, he thought, maybe this is for real.

But it couldn't be that easy.

Eve couldn't simply know that they were washed up. And she certainly didn't know that he had fallen in love with another woman.

And even if, in some vague, primitive way, she did know this, if it had miraculously communicated itself from him to her, he understood why she had walked out without at least one last try, one last fight, one last draining of their blood.

She was going away in a final effort to test him. Test herself, perhaps. Convince them both that life was not possible separately.

Chuck drained his cup of coffee.

It remained to be seen just who would be convinced of what.

But for the moment, he had no intention of sinking into a cycle of self-recrimination or analysis. The introspective way was not his dish. Thoughts and conclusions meant nothing. A guy could sit around all day planning to be brave … until the moment came.

No, what he thrived on was action.

And the action he intended to take right now was to the typewriter.

He got Bubber's fragment of manuscript from the living-room and shut himself into the den with the pot of coffee and his empty cup. The bare room with its cracked yellow walls seemed to bend kindly inward, encouraging concentration.

Reading through the script, he saw that Bubber's mind had been on other things. He pushed the papers into a wastebasket, deciding to do the whole thing from the beginning.

The quiet, the sense of solitude, the feeling that Eve was moving farther and farther away with each minute soothed Chuck into work. He patted little Minx and began typing fast, feeling that this one article would roll out all of a piece from a body and mind saturated with arguments and needing to manifest its constructive forces.

Night grew splendid and dark, curving its sheen of velvet sky around him. He sensed the small birds bedded down in the high trees and heard the coming to life of crickets rattling high and lively. Night meant sleep for some, work for others. Always the two faces reflecting a balance like scales weighing heaven and hell.

It was hardly midnight when Chuck finished. He recalled another room, another time some days before when night had presented itself as an early bird, waiting for him to grasp at it.

But he had blundered then. Blundered back into Eve. Blundered into the mistaken notion that he could be of help, that he could save them still.

Now all such notions were through.

The night was still young, yes. But he must keep his nose out of the dark corners.

He showered then and took fresh clothes from his valise.

Tonight, he must share what had happened with Robin. Maybe, if there were any sanity left in the universe, he could find the next step for her and for himself.

CHAPTER FIFTEEN

She told him, on the phone, not to come.

Her voice sounded too small, as though she were standing in a great church waiting for some awful retribution.

He did not argue.

But he drove to her house anyway and parked across the street to sit and contemplate the darkened windows. His first thought, the one that had brought him here in such haste, was that Barney had returned. Now he realized that this was foolish. No Barney, no Lil, no mortal person would have the power to cow Robin. She was walking alone in the company of her own conscience. Battling in the aftermath of revelation about Skinny.

He drove away to phone again the next day and the next. Yet each time, she turned him off. There was nothing he could do for her now. She must either swim to the surface and find air for herself or sink and drown among the losers.

Persistently, however, he visited Skinny, hoping that maybe Robin would turn up there in her own effort to deny the truth of what he had told her.

But she did not come.

She had rallied sufficiently to tell Skinny that she was not well. And, of course, she would not want him to see her with that banged up face.

Skinny himself seemed to be blossoming with the separation. They talked about cars and sports and school as though things were set up neatly as a math equation. For Skinny was making plans of his own.

"Know what I'm gonna do when I leap this jail?" Skinny said, tapping his fingernails against the brown bottle of pills beside him.

"What?" Chuck said, trying to muster interest.

"Rent my own room. Just like you did at my age. No more mamby pamby for me, no sir."

"Yeah? And what are you going to use for money?"

Skinny shrugged it off. "I can get a job."

"Doing what?"

"Gas station, at least. If I'm lucky, in a mechanics pit at the races."

"That means quitting school, doesn't it, kid?"

"You quit school."

"Who says I was so smart?"

Skinny grinned. "You got dough ... anything you want, Chuck. I say you're smart."

"Well, say again." Chuck lit a cigarette and dropped the match out of the open window, watching the wind take and spin it down to the asphalt of the parking lot.

"All right," Skinny said. "So tell me, what'd you miss?"

"The mellowing stage. You wouldn't know what I'm talking about just yet. But take it on faith, kid If school gives you nothing else, it keeps you off the streets long enough till you've aged in the wood a little."

Skinny looked disappointed.

"Besides, school makes opportunities."

"Like what?"

Chuck knew he could meet this sudden challenge. "Ever hear of the Sea Cresters, friend?"

"Who hasn't?" Skinny said. "What's that got to do with me?"

"Just this." But Chuck waited till Skinny looked primed for the clincher. "The guy who runs it, Ted Slats ..."

"I heard of him, too," Skinny said, urging him on.

"Then you know."

"Know what?" Skinny squealed with ill concealed tension.

"That Ted is on the verge of flunking algebra this year ... which means he won't graduate."

"Are you kidding?"

"Nope."

Chuck waited for the possibilities and connotations to sink in.

"How do you know?" Skinny said warily.

Chuck folded his arms with extreme casualness. "I was chinning with him just the other day. That snorkeling expedition? I forgot to tell you it was the Sea Cresters who went out. So, of course, Ted Slats and me buddied up. He kind of likes the idea of getting his name and the club's name in a magazine. Publicity, membership. You know the story. But he wouldn't want it getting out that his grades are lousy.... Follow?"

"I see," Skinny said. "That makes me the fixer-upper. I coach Ted in math. In exchange, he lets me into the Sea Cresters."

"How about it?" Chuck said. He knew he had Skinny in the bag. Now he tied the knot. "And since it's an all boys club, that automatically bars ... you know who."

Skinny rested back against the pillows, exhausted from the glitter of possibilities.

"Even so," he persisted, "I won't be able to swim for God knows how long."

"Somehow," Chuck said, "I doubt that. Swimming's just the thing to build a guy up. Darn sight better than exhaust fumes."

Chuck left Skinny this day feeling a sense of accomplishment. It bubbled up inside him so strong that there was nothing for it but to make Robin listen to him now. Make her realize that she needn't hide herself. That there was no shame in her misguided intentions toward Skinny. That Skinny would come through on top, if given half the chance.

He kept on ringing the doorbell.

She was home. He could feel her presence through the walls, knew that only her stubbornness prevented her from answering.

He rang again. He rattled the doorknob. He called her name. Then he walked around and squeezed through the bushes to the patio.

Robin lay on a sun chair, covered only by two narrow towels protecting the more delicate areas.

"Hello," Chuck said like an invited guest. "Fine weather, isn't it?"

Her skin shone with cocoa butter and he saw that her toenails were freshly polished. The old trimness he had seen that first day at the ralle was again in evidence.

Chuck sighed and sat down on the edge of another sun chair. He felt as though he would have to start all over again. He could sense the gates of her pulled shut against him. Closing off all the painful nerve ends. Preferring numbness to horror.

She smiled at him through the tinted lenses that cast bluish shadows on her cheeks. "You have such lovely manners," she said, her voice splashed with ice water.

The swelling had subsided from her lip. Her hair lay neat over the curve of her skull. Not a strand out of place. Not a thought out of place. Not a feeling out of place, Chuck knew.

"I don't care what you say," Chuck blurted. "But I want you to listen to me. And listen good." He leaned over, ignoring her own attempt to mock him now with the lowering lids behind the glasses.

"Don't bother," Robin said. "My ears turn off automatically when I hear a male voice."

"I know. You prefer Lil," he said bitterly.

He was being cruel. It was the only way now. He told her about the Sea Cresters and everything that had been said between him and Skinny earlier in the day.

Robin listened impassively.

"And since Skinny's coming home tomorrow, he's got to have the chance to build himself up a little. Put some color on that white skin so Ted Slats won't think I'm handing him a scarecrow."

"This all seems rather superfluous to me," Robin said.

"Not at all. Skinny may not know it, but he needs you now. You've got to pack up his things and take him away for a few weeks. Maybe to Carmel. Someplace quiet, where the living is easy and the water is good. Give him lots to eat, plenty of rest. A chance to muck around in the ocean a little."

"He won't want to go with me, Chuck. You were the first to tell me that."

"Sure," Chuck said, keeping cheerful. "That's how kids are. But he'll come with me."

"So take him. I won't object."

"That's not quite what I mean," Chuck said calmly. "Let's the three of us go someplace."

"So Jim can come home and tell his father what a rotter I am on top of all the rest that he thinks?" There was a grim smile around the edges of her lips.

Chuck shook his head. "You don't really believe that kid has a dirty mind."

"Frankly," Robin said, "I don't know what to believe by now. And it doesn't seem to make much of a difference, either. I've been thinking this through. Facing up to reality, as you would say, Chuck. I guess the best thing for me to do is pack my little toothbrush and thumb a ride."

Chuck let out a laugh. "You're still sounding like Eve."

In his excitement over Skinny, Chuck had forgotten to tell Robin the latest developments in his own domestic whirl. He spelled it out for her now, letting Robin amuse herself with private thoughts as he described their parting scene with a zest.

"That leaves you free, handsome, and at least twenty one," Robin said. "No wonder you're interested in a cozy little threesome. What's the matter, boy? Getting lonesome in that empty little bed at night?"

He hadn't thought about it.

"Maybe," Chuck said, tasting from her glass and finding that the ginger ale was unspiked.

"Well, count me out. Take Jim along if you think it will do him good. But let's just keep me off stage for a while, eh?"

"You don't understand anything," Chuck exploded. "All you want to do is sit there feeling sorry for yourself, broiling that skin till you turn into a hot dog." He shot up from the chair and shoved his hands deep into his pockets. "Well, that's just fine with me, sister. I'm sick of trying to jiggle you loose. Stay right where you are. Bury yourself if you want. I'm fed up with your cold potatoes."

"It's about time," Robin said, maintaining her blandness unshaken.

Chuck turned on his heel and swung through the house, unlocking the door with a force... She could keep it wide open from now on. He had no intentions of ever trying to break it down again.

Maybe he needed a new outlook. Something that sang, *To hell with dames altogether.*

The more you figured it, the more they didn't appreciate.

Goodbye, girlies.

Chuck slammed into the faithful little car and took off.

CHAPTER SIXTEEN

He careened down the road, veering around a taxi that was driving uphill.

The glimpse of a reddish gray head slipped along the periphery of his vision.

But his own thoughts rocketed before his eyes, driving out all contact with the surrounding elements.

It took five whole minutes to realize that he had seen Barney. By that time he was already at the bottom of the road and caught in the convergence of traffic moving both off and onto the freeway.

So what? he told himself.

Robin's life. Robin's business.

She liked getting smashed up. She must like it or else why did she stand still for it?

Blasted masochist.

Maybe she got her kicks by getting smacked around the walls.

He turned the car around. Then, with a fierce effort, pulled the wheel all the way so that he made a complete circle and continued moving in the direction away from Robin's house.

From now on, no more good Joe. All dames would come to him. Crawl over glass if necessary. No more complications. Easy love. Easy leave.

At Santa Monica beach, he thrashed around in the water, ate a soft shell crab sandwich and lay on his belly, digging his chin into one wrist and batting around the idea of catching a plane for New York.

Wouldn't that solve everything just fine?

First of all, it would throw Eve off the track for sure. Then, too, it would automatically cut off all thoughts of Robin, the temptation of her, from his mind.

The only trouble was that he had promises to keep. For all that he couldn't stomach Skinny, he couldn't chicken out now. That one brief glimmer of fire he had stirred in the boy couldn't be abandoned to the grizzly forces of his father. And Robin would certainly be of no use to the boy now.

Chuck turned over, kicking himself for playing such a damned saint. This wasn't his act. Nor his profession.

Well, he consoled himself, he could always leave after Skinny got settled back to school and launched with Ted Slats.

It was something to look forward to. And he needed something.

He strolled around the amusement park for the rest of the day, taking a couple of turns on the roller coaster, shooting some metal ducks for a quarter, pitching balls at pyramids of phony milk bottles.

When he got back home, the phone was ringing. He knew what it meant. Felt the inevitable and considered that a week for Eve was really a long time.

He let it ring.

It stopped finally and Chuck toyed with the idea of taking it off the hook.

Too soon to let Eve drag him back into captivity. Nor did he have the inclination for cutting her dead. From whom, he wondered, had he inherited such a lousy knack with women?

Intermittently, the phone rang through the night. He went out to a movie and came home to hear it ringing. Like a blood hound, it seemed to be chasing him down.

At last he decided that if the price of freedom meant going nuts or cutting off heads, then he would settle for cutting off heads.

So he waited till it rang again.

And this time he answered.

But it wasn't Eve at all. It hadn't been Eve all day or on into the night.

In his haste, Chuck left the receiver dangling. He felt a surge to run all the way to Robin rather than waste time starting up the car.

He thought about jail as he sped along, wondered what death felt like at that ultimate time. Considered what would be worse, life imprisonment or the chair.

But he had little time to consider.

When he burst through the door, Robin, stiff as a corpse herself, stood bent over the back of a wing chair, her hands clutching it. She said nothing and he had to go through the house looking for the thing he might have prevented.

He found the chubby little man, still dressed too warmly in his tweed suit, draped over the edge of the tub. The blood had ceased to flow, but the tub was stained with it. It clung to the porcelain, making congealed spots like a child's finger painting.

There was nothing Chuck could do except close the door and go back to Robin.

He had hardly noticed her before. Now he saw the bloody fingerprints all over her skin. She had pulled the terrycloth robe over her naked body and it too had blackish smears caught in its nubby threads.

Anything he might say would seem idiotic.

He unclasped her hands from the back of the chair and moved her around to sit down on it.

He tried to deduce what she might have done with the razor. Maybe … maybe it had been a struggle and then suicide? Maybe there was some saving grace on Robin's side?

"You weren't home all day long," she said dully. "Your timing is always ... so bad."

Chuck knelt beside her and took both her cold hands. "You've got to tell me what happened," he said gently.

"You know what happened."

Yes, he did know, really. He could imagine the violence starting up again, just as it had that other night. The forlornness and desolation in Robin's heart. And then the sudden surge of rebellion against Barney, goaded on by her hopelessness and sense of loss over the boy.

"But you didn't do it, did you?" Chuck said, still hoping.

"Of course I did," she answered, slowly coming awake again.

He could tell that she bobbed in and out of a dream.

"I did it with my own two, little hands," she said evenly. "And don't think for an instant, Chuck, that I'm sorry."

Her voice rang with truth.

"Well," he said, struggling, "it must have been self defense. I saw you beaten up before ..."

"As a matter of fact, it was. In a way."

"No jury would convict you."

"But they should."

"Robin, let's have no more self-destruction. Please."

She looked into his eyes, deep, deep. The cold container that held all her secrets seemed to be cracking wide open. "But this is what I've wanted for so many years," she murmured. "To kill a man like Barney. Since I was five years old and got my first mauling in a theater. Yes, ever since then, in one way or another, I've wanted to kill a man. To even up the score. In my own way, I've killed many men, just by not responding to them. By being cold and indifferent to their passion. And now," her voice broke a little, "I've finally done what I've dreamed of doing. I've killed a man, really. I've killed ... Barney."

She slumped forward and her arms went around his neck. He felt the warmth of her body, its yielding, its final acquiescence. Freed by her revenge, the hatred and the fight gone out of her, she could give of herself now. She could spring like a butterfly from its cocoon. And in giving of herself, she had come to him … not to Lil this time. Never again to Lil.

Chuck felt her lips against his neck, the pulse of her breathing beneath her robe.

"Don't," Chuck said gently. "You don't want this."

"But I do," she whispered. "I want to … so much. So much."

Her body seemed to demand his, reaching like a starved thing for him.

It was all wrong. The timing was cockeyed. He could not get the vision of Barney's mangled body out of his mind. And yet … It was now or never for them. Now … or never.

He dragged her up from the chair and into the kitchen. "We've got to clean you up," he said, struggling to be practical. "And think of a good reason why you didn't call the police directly after it happened."

"I don't care," she said, her eyes closing.

The weight of her hung from his neck.

For so many days he had desired this. Had needed her to crave him. And he had it now, spread out as an offering.

He wet a dish towel and stripped off her robe, letting it fall around her ankles.

She let him sponge her down. He moved the cloth over her chest and carefully over her breasts, trying to be mechanical, trying not to notice their roundness, the firm lifting of them so soft with a pattern of bluish veins contrasting with the bronzed color of her flesh.

"Don't play with me, Chuck," she said. "I'm so hungry for you."

He knew what she meant, knew what she felt.

"And anyway," she smiled now, finding her humor, "it would be sort of like my last supper."

Dripping with water, relaxed at last, wanting him openly, she seemed to transcend herself, taking Chuck with her into a private world, an Eden, secret and beautiful.

He stood up to meet the bending of her body toward him. Her lips, soft and salty with the wash of her own dried tears, met his mouth and clung to it.

Chuck lifted her slowly and carried her away to the alcove of the patio, where they would be alone, in the dark and far, far away from this house with its stark history.

She lay on her side, lifting her breasts to his lips, crooning gently as he found her.

The odor of soap where he had washed her cleansed her into freshness. She waved toward him like a new blade of grass growing upward. His arms encircled her waist and slipped along the smooth roundness of her buttocks. There was no space, no time, only this special dimension meant to be loved in.

She lifted her arms above her head and arched her body in a twisting motion so that she fit into his own nakedness now.

"Be gentle, darling," she said at first, sifting in her breath on the tightening of her lower lip.

He felt and reached and knew that she had not given herself often to men.

She might have been a virgin in his arms, or a wild thing from the woods, seeking him out of the inner calling of her own nature.

Crazily perhaps, he tasted in her body a trusting innocence. He knew this flesh had been given to him with bright confidence, with a belief that he would be good to it.

And so he reined in his passion until hers grew and blossomed, then he rode her carefully, taking her along with him to a profound eternity of pleasure filled to bursting.

They stayed locked together, separating for a few moments now and again, coming together once more, as though hating to part, as though separation could only let in an unwanted light.

The darkness blanketed their meeting, warming and cooling them by turns.

"Go slowly, darling..."

He knew he must create for her a loveliness to remember always.

And he gave of himself till dawn jeered jealously in through the windows.

CHAPTER SEVENTEEN

They dressed slowly together, as the inevitable spreading of light unrolled day like a carpet on which they must travel back to reality.

"You must eat something," Chuck said.

He felt tired, yet curiously vital. The thing that had to be done would be done. Somehow, they would deal with the inevitables and come out on top.

Of this he felt certain: that responsibilities could no longer destroy them.

It was as though a great, stifling hand had been lifted from their faces, allowing breath once more. Breath and life.

The flower of life fighting to grow in the midst of death.

"Are you hungry?" Robin said with a strange pleasure in her eyes. "Did I make you hungry?"

"Yes," Chuck said, touching her shoulder before it disappeared beneath the silk material of a blouse.

"Then I'll make you something to eat."

She seemed glad to do this and proceeded with elaborate arrangements, lifting a cold roast chicken from the refrigerator and filling two glasses with white wine.

"We'll have a celebration," she said, folding lime colored linen napkins beside place mats.

"To us," Robin murmured a few moments later, lifting her glass and smiling at him.

"To freedom," Chuck said.

"Yes," she nodded with something elastic and certain coming into her voice. "To freedom."

They ate in silence, sharing thoughts without needing to speak them. Sharing the moment that had passed and the burden, now to be lifted, of their future.

Relentlessly, the world outside came in to them. Cars taking children to school, delivery trucks clattering into driveways, someone calling to a neighbor about a garden hose.

Together, they listened to this hum of the day, sailing high above it, looking down with a first inkling of interest at the lives of others.

She did not need to say that it might have been like this for them, too. Nor did Chuck need to voice the burnished manliness reaching protectively toward Robin, toward all the mysteries of love that could flavor each trivial detail of a day with the taste of its exotic herb.

But at last they settled back, each with a cigarette, as though standing silent before a gigantic door that must be opened now and passed through to a nameless beyond.

"I want you to do something for me," Robin said at last.

"Of course," Chuck said, leaning comfortably back as she cleared the dishes.

"With no questions."

"All right."

"I want you to take Jim away with you today. Wherever you think it would be good."

"You mean directly from the hospital?"

"Yes."

He waited now, not asking the question, trusting her to do what she must.

Robin cleared her throat. Her back straightened a little as she sighed away from the sink. "After you leave me, I'm going to call the police. Whatever happens, I don't want Jim to be anywhere near. And I don't want you to be involved in it, either. You must take him and protect him, and if you can . . . explain to him someday what I tried to do for him."

"I'm sure he'll understand," Chuck said. He could not soothe her. Nor would he try.

"Understand?" Robin smiled, wielding a towel over a plate. "I don't understand myself."

"It'll work out," Chuck said, not like trying to placate a child with candy, but speaking the truth.

"Go now," she said. Her voice broke a little.

He did not try to prolong the moment. One couldn't drag out what needed to be settled right away. This he had learned with Eve.

"I'll take him to my place," Chuck said, rising from the table. "I'll get in touch with you when I can."

"Of course."

"And lawyers?"

"I know some."

There was nothing more to be said.

He kissed her on the mouth, lightly but long.

"Take care," he whispered.

"I love you," she said.

He saw that she had closed her eyes, needing for him to leave before she opened them again to the duty she must face.

With long strides, he got out of the house, tearing himself from the nearness of her, yet carrying with him the part that mattered, the intangible vibrations they had mingled to create a new substance now part of them both.

CHAPTER EIGHTEEN

He had hours yet before Skinny would need him at the hospital. Hours to kill or to build with.

Chuck went back to his house and stood in the center of his room, to stare at little Minx and wonder if the answers to all the riddles might not come forth in the arangements of letters to form meanings.

He sat down at the machine and typed ROBIN in the center of a page. What had he really understood of her? What did he understand now?

From hopelessness, she had created her own retribution. He wondered if the terrible thing that had happened could have been prevented if he had kept his mouth shut about Skinny's need to cut free from her attentions.

In a sense, what Robin had done was his own doing. The suppressed urge to violence had blossomed in her when she had ceased to feel useful.

Chuck's fingers roamed over the keys, typing out a complex dossier of Robin's personality as he had known it.

When the time came to leave for the hospital, he had barely started. He left the page in the machine and went to get Skinny.

The day, sealed in its glistening wrapper of sunshine, held struggles for Robin's soul that he would never know.

He imagined her down at the station now, telling her story to an alien face, repeating it to other faces,trying to make sensible details come to life for an attorney who would be sitting and sifting it through his logical mind.

The plea would be self-defense.

And, in truth, her action had been self-defense. A striking out against futility, against denial, against the emptiness of sham.

He could only hope that the lawyer would see the backlog of complexities that absolved Robin.

Chuck's thoughts strayed to New York and the contacts he had there. He hardly realized that he had reached the parking lot of the hospital.

In his room, Skinny waited, his few things zippered into an overnight bag.

Skinny looked even thinner than Chuck had remembered. Dark circles aged his eyes. Sharp cheekbones made knife like edges in his face.

"Hi," Chuck said not too brightly. He didn't want to give the kid false leads.

"Hi," Skinny said.

"I'm the welcoming committee," Chuck said, lifting the bag.

"That's fine by me."

No questions about Robin.

"Let's go." Chuck opened the door. "Do I have to sign out for you or what?"

At the desk, Chuck went through a routine of papers, making facile explanations where necessary, oiling himself for all the other explanations he would in time have to go through with Skinny.

In the car, Chuck said, "How about a malted?"

And at the soda fountain, he told Skinny that they were going to his place instead of home.

In the chocolate sweet atmosphere, Chuck's voice sounded almost too casual. A jukebox blared something rock and roll, making his statement an easy, breezy matter.

Skinny sipped at his malted. He seemed not to be listening.

"Hey, get with it, man," Chuck said, impatient for Skinny to start becoming suspicious.

"Look," Skinny said, coming up from his own thoughts, "if we're not going directly home, do I get five minutes to make a phone call?"

"Sure," Chuck said, surprised.

He watched Skinny amble down to the line of booths, trying to figure what secrets a kid like Skinny could possibly have.

But when Skinny returned, his face alight and bursting with anticipation, Chuck knew he wouldn't have to wait long for the answer.

Skinny slid back onto the wooden seat.

"All fixed?" Chuck said.

"Yep."

Now Skinny dawdled over his malted, playing with the straws, edging up to his confession.

"Look," Skinny stammered, "there's someone coming here I want you to meet."

His pale face flushed a bit, outlining the soft beginnings of his beard.

Suddenly it was all clear to Chuck. He remembered Skinny's evasion about an earlier phone call and the look of guilt on his face then. Chuck leaned back and relaxed against the plastic upholstery. His eyes wandered to the counterman, scraping bacon grease from the grill, then back to Skinny's mouth tightening with the suppression of his excitement and anticipation.

"Is she nice?" Chuck ventured.

Skinny's flush deepened. "I think so."

"A girl from school?"

"How'd you guess?"

Skinny's kidlike surprise amused Chuck. "One man just knows about another, isn't that so?"

"Sure," Skinny said, considering the prospect of a cigarette. "That's so."

Perhaps ten minutes later, Chuck followed Skinny's widening gaze to the doorway.

He felt his palms growing cold at the sight of the girl sidling in.

She couldn't be more than sixteen but the makeup on her face covered all youth, all freshness. She wasn't chewing gum but she ought to have been. Her wide, petulant mouth parted in greeting as she spotted Skinny. Pushing her sweater-molded breasts outward, she bounced toward the table.

Every eye in the place followed the movement of her behind. The outline of underwear showed beneath her tight skirt, pegged to curve along her high buttocks and cling to her thighs. She wore sandals that laced halfway up her calf.

Chuck withheld a whistle. His mind flicked over whether or not Robin had known about this girl in Skinny's life. Maybe Skinny didn't have the guts to tell her. Or if he had, in innocence, Robin must have tried in vain to break it up before Skinny got taken for too steep a ride.

"Chuck," Skinny said, rising to let the girl slide in beside him, "this is Mindy Lou."

"Most folks call me Lou," she said to Chuck, lifting the great weight of her hair and draping it over one shoulder toward the Saint Christopher medal swinging between her breasts. "That's because I'm rather boyish."

Chuck sensed instantly that she was flirting with him. No doubt she wouldn't have bothered coming out today if Skinny hadn't told her there was someone he wanted her to meet.

"I'll call you Mindy, if that's okay," Chuck said, trying to strike the right note between cool distance and friendliness for Skinny's sake. He would have to work at keeping Skinny from losing face with her.

"Suit yourself," Mindy said and leaned over to suck up the last of Skinny's malted.

"What're you drinking?" Chuck said.

"They don't serve it here," she answered with a wink.

Skinny put his arm around her shoulder. She looked at his dangling fingers and sighed at Chuck with a surfeit of boredom.

"Skin hasn't been well," she sighed. "We must be nice to him."

"Oh, I'm in great shape now."

Comments from other tables were reaching them and Skinny, overhearing them, mistook their meaning and gleamed with pride.

"If you're not drinking," Chuck said abruptly, "we might as well go."

"Where to?" Mindy said, fingering her medallion.

"To Chuck's place," Skinny said. His tone said: Where there are no parents.

Mindy eyed Chuck. "You live alone, do you?"

"Of course he lives alone," Skinny answered.

Chuck realized that Skinny had never met Eve. Didn't even know he was married.

"Then we can have a ball," Mindy said, "... maybe."

Chuck snapped up the check and went to pay it while Skinny took the girl to the car.

On top of all his troubles, there was this damned girl now. He considered Mindy and realized that for a guy like Skinny, something like her was inevitable. She could wind him around her finger. Compliments ... cash ... an escort on dull nights ... general houseboy and handyman. While Skinny lapped it up.

Chuck drove them all back to the house while Mindy sat in the back ignoring all of Skinny's chatter about cars and the Sea Cresters. At least, Chuck consoled himself, Skinny hadn't forgotten himself altogether.

The house, once all lonely solitude, was now all blastings of radio that Mindy found and snapped on.

She began showing Skinny how to do the twist, at the same time indicating to Chuck her ability to do other things not too distantly related.

Chuck saw that Skinny was nabbed and it made him sick.

"Do you dance, Chuck?" Mindy invited.

"Never," Chuck lied.

"Chuck's a sportsman," Skinny explained.

"There's all kinds of sport," Mindy hinted.

It was the last straw.

Chuck went to her and grabbed her by the wrist. "Look, devil," he said. "Skinny and I have a lot to do today. I'm taking you home."

"Hey, Chuck," Skinny squealed in protest. "What's biting you?"

"Nothing's bit me yet," Chuck said calmly. "And nothing will."

In the brunt of Skinny's indignation, he yanked Mindy from the livingroom, feeling in her pretense of opposition that she was all too willing to get away from Skinny.

She flopped with mock indignation in the seat and yanked the rear view mirror around, checking the line of her lipstick.

Chuck twisted the mirror back and spurted the car downhill, so that Mindy's head snapped backward.

"You're a rough one," she said.

"Take it easy, sister," Chuck said. "I'm not Skinny."

"Don't I know. And don't I like it," she drawled.

Grimly, Chuck kept his eyes on the road.

But hardly a moment later, he felt her hand creeping along his thigh.

"You wanted to be alone with me, didn't you?" she said, laughing, ignoring her hand as though it belonged to someone else.

"Not particularly," he said. "I don't rob cradles."

"When did you ever see this kind of baby in a cradle?" she replied, undaunted.

The thick odor of her sweet perfume filled the car. Chuck rolled down a window.

"Now, don't play hard to get, Chuck. 'Cause I always get it anyway."

"You'll get it, all right," Chuck spat. "Right in the neck."

"Fine by me," she said. Her hand slipped between his legs. "Let's neck."

He let go of the wheel with one hand and slapped her hard, as he had slapped Robin and sensed the same futility of it.

"You bastard," she breathed. "I could sew you up in jail for statutory rape any time I please."

"Just try it," he said, calling her bluff. "And if you don't shut up, I'll throw you out right here and let you walk home."

This settled her back into a more docile condition.

"Does Skinny's mother know you've been muzzling with him in the bushes?"

"I only met her once," she answered sullenly.

"I gather you two didn't hit it off."

"She warned me to stay away from her kid, the crazy bitch."

"And you told this to Skinny?"

"Sure," she said. "Is he a man or a mousenik?"

Chuck hung onto the wheel, fighting with himself against giving this nut something to remember.

But it made perfectly clear sense to him now why Skinny didn't care if he never saw Robin again.

He dropped the girl off in front of her house with the tacit understanding that she was out of Skinny's life for good.

Then he spun to go, aware that the job he had to do for Robin was bigger, more complicated than he had expected.

CHAPTER NINETEEN

But the world wasn't standing still until Chuck could get things sorted out with Skinny.

A telegram had arrived in his absence. He tore open the envelope while Skinny sulked in the livingroom.

It said: CAN I PLEASE COME HOME ALL MY LOVE ALWAYS EVE

With exactly ten words she was ready to start all over again. Snap them back to the primitive days of their misery.

With exactly ten words she was threatening him, daring him to deny her, implying perfect contrition that expected a correspondingly perfect forgiveness.

Chuck muttered something obscene and crumpled the paper, flinging it into the sink. It bounced up and rolled away on the floor.

Eve's threat boiled in his blood. If he answered anything but the expected reply, she would do something dramatic. Something to frighten Bubber enough so that Bubber would bring her home and dump her on the doorstep.

Chuck dug into one pocket and rattled three dimes against a nickel. "Skinny," he called, "come on in here."

He heard Skinny's reluctant footsteps.

"I thought you were a right guy, Chuck," Skinny said, his voice heavy with disappointment.

"Don't worry," Chuck said. "It's always darkest just before it's totally black."

"Sure," Skinny said. "When're you taking me home?"

"You want to go home?" Chuck snapped.

"What the hell's the difference between home and here?"

The sight of Skinny's long face, the feel of Eve's ghost hanging tearfully over him, the knowledge of Robin someplace in a small desolate room . . . all these jelled to drive out the remains of Chuck's patience.

"You want to know the difference?" Chuck shouted. "Sit down and I'll tell you."

He gave it to the kid straight, sparing no detail about his father, about Robin, or about Mindy Lou. In three hours, he made Skinny do all the growing up that should have been spread over the past five years of his adolescence.

When he had finished, Skinny's face had gone a sickly gray. He got to the sink and retched up his insides as though to spit out and thereby negate the truth of Chuck's words.

"Nobody comes into this world with a guarantee to be coddled," Chuck said gently, holding the boy's neck. "Neither kings nor paupers."

He put Skinny to bed then, forced him to swallow a sedative from the bottle of pills he had brought home from the hospital and went back to clean up the mess.

Skinny slept hard through the night and Chuck pounded on the typewriter while the stars grew brilliant, then paled away into dawn.

Chuck tiptoed into the room with a glass of warm milk. Skinny twisted on the bed, coming awake as though poked alive by the burning sensation of hot coals.

"I got to see her," Skinny mumbled. "Got to . . ."

Chuck quieted him and made him swallow the milk.

So do I, he was thinking.

But he knew that Robin wasn't ready yet to face either one of them.

They talked about it some more, Chuck easing Skinny little by little into a grasp of profundities, of heart secrets, of questions about women. He spoonfed Skinny with the knowledge that he had, believing it would turn someday into useful nutriment.

"She always wanted to be the best for you," Chuck said. "And I think you owe it to her now."

"Owe what, Chuck?"

"First, that you don't hate her."

"I can't help it," his voice rasped. "I hate her with every gut in me. And my father, too. I hate them both. You just don't know how much I..."

"Enough," Chuck interrupted. "The point is, are you going to sit around here and wallow in it or are you going to do something about yourself, for a change?"

"I've got to see her," Skinny repeated. "Got to see her face to face. Hear it from her own mouth what she did to him. What she meant to do when she..."

He couldn't finish the sentence.

"Well, you'll have to take it from me for the time being."

"I don't have to take anything from anybody anymore," Skinny answered bitterly.

"That's even better," Chuck smiled, going to open the windows.

"The phone's ringing," Skinny said.

Chuck listened, torn between answering and letting it pass. Once before he had let it pass. And now, if Robin wanted him... needed him...

With a sudden dash, he made it to the hall and grabbed up the receiver.

"... Didn't you get my telegram, Chuckie?"

Chuck slammed down the phone.

"Who was it?" Skinny asked anxiously.

"Nobody," Chuck said in a dull voice.

"Whatdaya mean, nobody?"

Chuck lit another cigarette. His tongue tasted thick with the residue of nicotine. "Just a no good dame," he said.

"Lou?"

"No, not Mindy."

Skinny waited, his eyes demanding an answer. If Chuck didn't answer him now, if he evaded, all the things he'd been saying to Skinny stood in jeopardy of not being trusted, not being accepted.

"Only my wife," Chuck breathed.

Skinny's lips parted. "Your . . ."

"That's it, kid," Chuck said with a wry humor.

Skinny's fingers twisted into one end of the pillowcase. "You mean to tell me that you're married?"

"Um hmm."

"Jeeezus," Skinny breathed. "Who would ever have thought . . ."

". . . that the great Chuck Tatum got stuck?"

Skinny only blinked.

Chuck sat down on the edge of the mattress. "I bet you thought that hell was reserved for you, eh, kid?" Skinny tried a weak smile. "You know what, Chuck?"

"What?" Chuck said absently as he felt the pressure of Eve closing in again.

"I think we both need to get away from things for a while."

"Amen," Chuck said. And then, because he couldn't just sit still to let Robin swim as she might in the turmoil so overwhelmingly strong against her, he added, "Say, how would you like to take a trip with me for a couple of days?"

"Sure," Skinny said. "But where to?"

"New York, of course," Chuck replied.

And his ears closed off against any objection Skinny might make. Closed, because he knew he had to go and kill off, once and for all, some of the little rats nibbling quietly away at his life.

CHAPTER TWENTY

New York was Chuck's town.

With the snow driving hard and the drab gray of houses packed together, crowding out the sky, New York meant power, success, the playing of people, who played one in turn, for the stakes of the great game.

Skinny shivered. He huddled into the heavy coat Chuck had bought him and cupped his hands over his reddening ears. He squinted at Chuck as they crossed the air field and said, "Is this for real?" His words whipped off on a whining of wind.

Chuck dragged him through the vestibule and out the other side into a cab.

He told the driver an address in downtown Manhattan, then settled back to watch Skinny breathing on his frozen fingertips.

"Catch yourself a cold," Chuck said, "and I'll break your neck."

"Well, there's one advantage, anyway," Skinny consoled himself.

"Yeah, what?"

"No school."

Chuck grinned. "Don't kid yourself." It was all planned out for Skinny, whether he liked it or not. And school came later in the schedule. School and swimming and cars again. The things a kid should have. With a girl friend thrown in, too. The things a man should have.

They climbed four dingy flights of a sagging tenement house and Chuck unlocked the door of a pleasant black and white painted apartment with windows that looked out onto naked, swaying clotheslines.

"This yours?" Skinny said, eying a hi-fi and the wall of books.

"Bubber's," Chuck said. "Remember him?"

"Oh, yeah," Skinny said, folding himself into a sling chair. "That fat guy."

While Skinny got up again, sidled around, poured himself a taste of brandy, Chuck got down to business.

Half an hour later, with Skinny safely tucked away for a nap, Chuck was out again and on his way to the lawyer that handled all his troubles from way back when some wise guy had tried to clip a couple of bucks on a slander case over one of his articles.

"Guthrie," Chuck said to the pin stripe suited man leaning back in his swivel chair behind a sweeping gray mustache, "hang onto your briefcase, this is going to be a long trip."

Chuck poured it out.

He waved off all objections to a divorce and made provisions for a suitable financial arrangement.

That was the business end.

It took him a minute to get his guts together and let loose with the real cause of his flying to New York.

How do you tell a man, a professional man, about so subtle and evasive a personality as Robin?

Chuck tried.

When he had finished, Guthrie made some long distance calls. One to San Francisco and two to Los Angeles.

"We'll do what we can," Guthrie said. "We might expect a recommendation of leniency. But beyond that, I would not attempt to say."

"That's it?" Chuck said.

"Yes."

It had been a long trip, powered by great hopes. But now Chuck felt that it had all been for nothing. He surveyed an ivy plant on the windowsill behind Guthrie's back and his glance passed on to the mist of jagged buildings, suddenly so cold, so indifferent to human needs for survival.

"Thanks, anyway," Chuck said.

He walked the streets for a while, letting the snowflakes drift in to melt around his neck. New York was supposed to have been his push button, his gimmick to right all the little electric trains gone off the track. Now he felt foolish as a kid for having expected Santa Claus to come down the chimney personally.

But he stuck it out with Skinny for a week, taking him around town, introducing him to the men whose by-lines he knew from various sports magazines.

For Skinny, it was a vacation.

For himself, it was a guitar with broken strings trying to make a melody play where none was possible.

And always, always, the thundering need to see Robin rattling like a trip hammer against the tissue of his inner ear. Something in him seemed to be waiting for a signal, for the right moment in time, before he would go to her, as he knew he must.

It had broken all over the papers, of course. And keeping Skinny in New York helped, at least, to keep him clear of the scandal, the news lechery of photographers.

Without Skinny knowing it, they were hiding out in New York, really, until the nasty winds died.

But it was Skinny himself who suggested it one night when they had come home from a roller derby.

"Look, Chuck," he said, pulling off one of the two sweaters he wore against the cold, "we're only marking time here, aren't we?"

"You think so?"

"I know what you're waiting for," Skinny said. "You're waiting for me to get over this kick I'm on."

"Which kick?" Chuck said, swigging from a bottle of beer.

"The hate kick."

"Well?"

"Well, I give up, don't you see? I mean, I've been thinking about it, deep down in the back of my head somewhere. Thinking and thinking till it wore itself clean out."

"You mean that?"

Skinny grinned. "What could I do? I put up a good fight, but I lost. I can't ever hate anything for very long."

Chuck sensed the boy's honesty. And he knew how the mind could work to soothe things over. Skinny was young, he couldn't mourn forever. The very nature of life was regeneration.

"You know what I want to do?" Skinny said. "I want to go back home and see Mom. I want to tell her that..." he struggled to keep his voice steady. "... I'm rooting for her."

Chuck realized that these were the very words he had been waiting to hear. If he had been of no use to Robin in any other way, he knew at least that he had helped her with the boy.

"All right, Jim," he said, tacitly acknowledging the boy's arrival at manhood, "we'll catch a flight first thing in the morning."

But restful sleep would not come to Chuck. He had been living too long off his nerves, pushing himself along a wire of tension.

How much was there still to be done? The question spun dizzily in his head as the night ticked on. Around him he could feel loose ends dangling. He stretched in restless dreams to catch them and pull them down.

He felt with an animal's premonition that he had not yet heard the last from Eve. That somewhere she waited to trap him again.

And Robin... Robin's face looked down at him from a distance unreachable, smiling at him, needing to be touched, needing the sustenance of his nearness.

Chuck came awake to the drifting of dismal flakes melting on the windowsill. He sat up in Bubber's bed, knowing that to return to California meant to run smack into the full brunt of all troubles.

He sighed and swung his naked feet to the cold linoleum.

CHAPTER TWENTY-ONE

From halfway down the hill, Chuck could see that his house was not empty. The windows, once curtained, stared nakedly into the sun, daring it to penetrate their secrets.

Chuck stopped the car.

"Look, kid," he said, "I got things that need doing up there. Alone."

"I can face anything you can face," Skinny said with conviction. He was leaning out the window, greedily soaking up the warmth drained from his spare body in New York.

"Sure," Chuck said. "But this has got nothing to do with you and I don't want you to get mixed up in it."

Before Skinny could argue, he swung the car around and made a phone call to Ted Slats.

He left Skinny with Ted at a drugstore, confident now that the two boys would hit it off. Skinny was a right guy, now that he had learned not to feel so sorry for himself.

Then, with the calm bleakness of a growing storm, Chuck returned to face whatever he must at the cottage.

The front door was closed but not locked and he pushed it open.

"Eve," he called with loud force. "Where the hell are you?"

No answer.

He stepped into the livingroom and into chaos.

The log table stood on its side, one ragged curtain still hung crookedly. Another piled in a crumple on the rug, stained with a yellowish substance that looked like raw eggs broken and smeared around. Their wedding snapshot lay scattered in bits. A deep rent in the sofa ended at the point of a paring knife still stuck in the foam rubber.

Chuck dashed into the bedroom to find more of the same. Cracks radiated like a sunburst from the dressing table mirror. A broken perfume bottle lay in smithereens on the lacquer eaten away in rivulets by the alcohol content.

His stomach had turned into a steel band. He pressed the palms of his hands together, needing to steady himself, not yet able to predict whether supreme anger or supreme horror would culminate his search.

"Eve!"

More silence. Yet a silence that thundered.

With sudden knowledge of the processes that made the machine of her mind go haywire, he raced to the den, to the one room he had cautioned her not to enter without knocking.

The first thing he saw was little Minx, shattered and spilled across the floor, type arms twisted, case dented in as though some venomous demon had taken an axe to it.

He heard a little laugh. Something like the cry of a kitten in the night.

She sat in one corner of the room all folded into a tiny ball of flesh. Her hair, tangled and damp, covered her face so that only a bit of nose poked through.

He dashed at her, grabbed her shoulders, and started shaking.

She went limp in his arms and he knew. The sweet smell that filled the house heavy as incense was not her perfume at all.

No. As he watched her eyeballs roll to reveal only their bluish whiteness, he knew that Barney had left her a legacy that night. Barney had opened doors for Eve through which she might never return. She had an addiction now, finally, stronger than her marriage.

Chuck went to the phone and called an ambulance. Then he saw, for the first time, a yellow page scribbled on in Bubber's writing.

It said: I couldn't make it, man. She doesn't want anything but you. Good luck.

Chuck crumpled the paper and bounced it off the wall. For an instant, he felt the arrow of Eve's need zinging right smack into the center of his forehead, praying, begging that he help her. He realized that without the power of his confidence, she might never find the incentive to give up the new found escape into drugs.

His chest constricted with pain.

"Eve," he said, but it was a whisper now. A whisper on the wind to a ghost who could never respond.

He went in and sat with her on the couch until the internes arrived and took her from him.

As the ambulance pulled away, Chuck shook himself. It felt like shaking flies off the open, bleeding wound of his body.

He had loved her.

In his way, he still loved her.

It was like loving death and the taste of goodbye was of salt.

For awhile, he was not quite sure. But then his legs carried him on, moving him to where he must go, to where he could still be of help . . . to where he wanted to be.

He went to get Skinny at the drug store.

"You know," Skinny said in the car, "he's not a bad guy."

"Ted?" Chuck said dully.

"Yeah, Ted. . . . Say, what are you thinking about, anyhow?"

What he was thinking about made no difference, Chuck knew. It was only what he did that counted, that could ever count.

He traced Robin to where they were keeping her pending the date of her trial.

It was a spare building, making no pretense of home or comfort. Tan walls and dusty floors did not welcome visitors with gladness.

And Chuck could only hope that Robin would see him now. That she was ready, as Skinny was ready to face her.

But they would not let Skinny in and Chuck knew he had to be the courier, the messenger of hope.

He hoped that Robin would believe him now about good tidings, as she had believed him about bad.

He waited an eternity, knowing that they would have but a few minutes together, tightening himself to get it all said in the face of ebbing time.

He saw her then, dressed in something that did not quite fit. The clothes were her own but she had lost so much weight that they hung impossibly. Yet the lean grace of her figure could not be disguised nor the life in her eye extinguished.

When she saw him, her pale lips smiled, her arms reached out. And Chuck knew she would listen.

"Has it been too rough?" he said.

"Not terribly. You know, talking and talking about it ... the lawyer always wants to know if I've forgotten something ... is sort of like being in church."

"The confessional?" Chuck said, hoping to be lighthearted for her.

"No," she said. "Rather like seeing ..." But she did not finish. She merely stopped in the middle of her thought and let her eyes feed on him hungrily. "I'm glad you came to me," she said at last.

"I'm not alone," Chuck said. "They wouldn't let Jim in, he's under age. But he told me to tell you that he's rooting for you, Robin."

His words made a ring around the two of them. Something bright and golden and shining.

"We love you," he whispered. "However long it takes ... we love you."

They didn't say much after that. They merely sat together, feeling the minutes pass, minutes that would grow over the chasm of their circumstance and lower a bridge one day, on which they would walk from opposite sides, to meet, to touch again, and to begin …

"Time's up."

But the guard's voice did not separate them. Not really.

"I'll come tomorrow," Chuck said.

"Yes, Chuck. Tomorrow."

He did not turn, but he knew that she was watching him move down the corridor. And that when she could no longer see him, she would listen to the sound of his footsteps.

Skinny waited in the car.

"So?" Skinny said anxiously.

"So what did you expect?" Chuck said, thrusting the little Morris into gear. "We've got to get on back to your house and start cleaning things up. Or do you want your mother coming home to a mess?"

It was early in the day. Early … and they had plenty of time.

www.ingramcontent.com/pod-product-compliance
Lightning Source LLC
LaVergne TN
LVHW051002080826
845145LV00009B/2422